The alien was a member of the ruling class—a gameplayer. He felt a good measure of satisfaction as this project neared its end. Already the portion of his planet's fleet assigned to him was on its way to Earth.

Although he had almost all the information he needed, there were still some blank areas that should be filled in before he ordered a completion. He still had to finish building up an acceptable game picture of human beings at work and at play. This should not prove to be too difficult, even though he had had the bad luck of drawing a seemingly illogical race for his first species-destroying game.

His final report to the committee would make him look like a perfect gameplayer. . . . Yet there was something nagging at him from the back of his very complex mind—he had the feeling that this particular race ought to be destroyed quickly, no matter what his game report looked like. . . .

A. E.
VAN VOGT

THE
ANARCHISTIC
COLOSSUS

ace books
A Division of Charter Communications Inc.
A GROSSET & DUNLAP COMPANY
1120 Avenue of the Americas
New York, New York 10036

THE ANARCHISTIC COLOSSUS

Copyright © 1977 by A. E. van Vogt

An ACE Book, by arrangement with the author.

Printed in U.S.A.

INTRODUCTION
By: A. E. van Vogt

In this novel I took it for granted that the basic nature of, particularly, the human male, as it has been observed from ancient times, is not about to alter for the better. And so, my question was not: how much perfection may we anticipate from human beings in the future? It was: what kind of technology would be required to maintain a system of anarchism among all those misbehaving human beings around us? No government. No police. Nobody minding the store. The entire operation would, of course, have to be automatic.

Surely—you say—science fiction, which all too often tends to create its own facts to bolster the reality of a story premise, has finally gone too far. Meaning, even to pose such a question is ridiculous. Human beings are incorrigible in their endless dangerous madness.

I agree. That's exactly what I said. Now, how can we have an anarchistic society in spite of that madness?

Well!

As I write this, I have before me a copy of a patent issued several years ago to a major west coast aircraft corporation. In it the Kirlian photography technology is combined with a relay system, whereby the following occurs: The camera focuses.

The person photographed—an actor—pretends anger. His realistic evocation of the emotion alters the Kirlian pattern. Which triggers a relay. Across the building, in another room, a second relay shuts off (or turns on) a large machine.

Two thoughts here as an aside. First: All too often when science fiction writers of 1977 predict the future, they come up with something that was invented in 1967. We have a little bit of that here. The second aside: Recently, I read that a group of American scientists have belatedly proved that the Kirlian Effect cannot be achieved without the aid of moisture—and therefore it is not what was claimed. I can only look at my copy of the foregoing-described patent—and shake my head over their disproof.

The patent establishes that a machine can be controlled by a photographed human emotion. I believe that, for story purposes, I am entitled to deduce that if one emotion—anger—can be used for one purpose, then a spectrum of other emotions could, by way of microprocessors—tiny computers—perform a large number of coordinated actions.

We may therefore visualize a unit, complete with its own tiny computer and its Kirlian sensors, plus a laser penalty system (which last also constitutes the unit's own defense system). Visualize this additionally multiplied by one or more billion duplicates of each other, all self-sustaining but inter-connected, and, of course, scattered all over the planet. At which point you have the condition on earth when my story opens.

. . . The alien invaders looked over this ideal society. And deduced that anarchistic man could not defend his planet.

ONE

IT IS NOT EASY for some one or some thing in a distant (multi-light-years away) part of the universe to watch a single episode of human existence on earth. But the problems of such a spy operation are within the frame of physics. And so that somebody—who possessed that high a level of scientific achievement, and was sufficiently motivated to spend the time and the energy—had his awareness focussed just above human head level. Meaning just over six feet above the ground.

What was visible seemed scarcely worth the effort. A tree-lined residential street of a large city. Night. The only mobile life form in sight was a man strolling along on the sidewalk. He was coming *toward* the point of focus. So it would almost seem as if he were the object of the remote being's interest.

The man coming along the street could have been an earth scientist, or some other professional type. He seemed about forty earth years old, and had a middle-class appearance—that is, he was dressed in a suit, and was clean-shaven. He looked intelligent.

Nothing more was visible.

But additional developments were not long in coming.

As the night stroller came full under the street

light, there was an unexpected movement in the hedge beside the sidewalk. It was a tiny rustling sound of leaves and boughs scraping against each other.

The next instant a young man burst forth from the darkness of the hedge. Without a word, he launched himself at the older man. The victim had half-turned at the sound. But he was obviously not prepared for violence. Obviously, because the first rush of the assailant caught him and nearly knocked him over. And then he was being struck with fists that did not hold back, and shoved even harder.

He fell. And that was the purpose. Down on top of him, with knees into the victim's groin, plunged the assailant. The attacker's hand reached inside his own jacket. A syringe flashed, as the hand came into the open. The young man—for that was what he was—thrust it downward. He was clearly and without pause intending to inject something into the body of the man whom he had struck down so forcefully.

He was not successful.

There was an interruption.

At that precise instant of time, the two—the attacker and the attacked—had a synchronized reaction to . . . something.

Whatever the perception was, it caused the attacker to hesitate.

The victim, though he was down and on his back—and though he gave the appearance of being helpless—now, belatedly, showed that he was at least partially capable of defending himself.

A tiny beam of light reached up from his right lapel and touched the syringe.

The brightness of it sparkled and coruscated, almost like a hair-thin stream of water splashing. As this stream of light splashed, it broke up into the colors of the rainbow.

The youth uttered a moan. The syringe fell from his suddenly nerveless fingers. For a moment he crouched there, knelt there, blanked out by pain.

For that moment, he looked like an overgrown teenager, blond and blue-eyed, with the only disparate factor being his size. He had the build of a football player. He was an inch taller than his intended victim. He looked as if he weighed 190 pounds.

As he cringed, held by uncontrollable physical agony, he had the helpless appearance of someone who could be picked off by a sharpshooter, and in fact he was a perfect target for the sedation method of the Kirlian computer system that protected the city. And, of course, his victim could have reacted with more of that numbing light.

For whatever reason, apparently none of these things happened during the split-instants that he could not move.

Moments after that, the youth showed *his* power. He straightened. He said aloud, "Hank!"

A voice spoke out of his coat collar. "Yeah?"

"It's a robot. This is a trap."

"You're loaded for anything, boy," said the same bodiless voice, "so don't leave yet. How do you know it's a robot?"

"When I kneed him, his abdomen felt—you know—not human."

"Okay! Talk to him! What's the trap for?"

No one had moved . . . much. The erstwhile victim continued to lie on his back, and continued to have the appearance of a middle-aged, middle-class professional man. And the attacker remained in a kneeling position on top of him.

He seemed a little grimmer, as he said, "Okay, talk!"

"The trap," replied the robot, calmly, "is designed to identify you and to find out why you haven't triggered the Kirlian scanners of this city."

"What are you authorized to do to get that information?" asked the blond youth.

"To hold you. I have already notified a Tech volunteer."

"The message to the volunteer didn't get through," said the powerful young man, "so my question is still, how much force are you authorized to use?"

"Only what I need to defend myself, hold you, and call a volunteer."

"Since you can do none of those things, I'll just get up and we'll separate."

"I'm supposed to hold you," said the robot, "so we can't separate."

The youth stood up. "That's no problem," he said. "We understand those kinds of forces. Where's your human look-a-like, Frank Corman?"

"Home—watching and listening."

The human being laughed curtly. "He may be home, but he's getting no picture and no sound. Goodbye!"

He stepped toward the hedge. There was the same crackling and rustling of leaves and branches. The next instant he was through, and gone into the darkness beyond.

With his reference point—the youth—retreating,

the alien watcher had progressive difficulty maintaining his viewpoint on the street. The scene flickered and grew darker. But he was able to observe that the robot rolled over, picked up the syringe, climbed to his feet, and said, "Mr. Corman."

"What happened?" came a voice that seemed to be an exact duplicate of the robot's. It spoke from the region of the robot's stomach. "We lost contact."

"I have the syringe," was the reply.

"Oh, good. Now, we'll be able to find out what he intended to do to me. Get over here, quick!"

The scene and the voice were faint and faraway. The alien abruptly gave up on it—and rejoined the fleeing blond youth.

Contact was swift. The young human being (for those who understood complex life structures—and the alien did) was the mobile relay unit on earth for his communication system. All the neural wiring and the organic control switching centers in the spine and braincase constituted existent equipment of a quality that could not be duplicated by machinery.

The attacker was visibly a young man in a hurry. He raced across one darkened yard and onto a bright street, then over another yard and past a large house, and so to a second street.

There, a car with a man at the wheel waited at a curb. As the youth came up, breathless, the driver leaned over and opened the door. For a few moments as he poised there in that bent-over position, *his* face was brightened by a street light. It showed him to be a man in his middle thirties. The face, thus revealed, was not an intellectual type. But it had a certain openness and the kind of maturity that comes from an intensive education in the university of experience and from many, many decisions.

His face (and head and shoulders) withdrew into the unlighted shadows, as his young companion scrambled into the car and shut the door. The vehicle was in motion even before he could settle down. It glided forward and away from the curb making only a faint tire sound and soft hissing noise.

For the alien, the movement of the car was another opportunity to evaluate human technology in everyday life, although it was not easy to immediately determine the motive power of the car at this colossal distance. He deduced it was a turbine engine. The smooth, silent, flowing power had that feel to it. Was hydrogen gas the heating element? It was difficult to be sure. He would have to wait for a chance word, or other clue.

The information was important because after the game player had played his game to its grim conclusion, he was expected to make a report that would show thorough knowledge of the doomed race.

Inside the moving vehicle an urgent dialogue began swiftly. The youth said, "How do you figure what happened? A trap?"

The man—Hank—was cool. "The Techs know something is wrong. You've beaten up top-rated Techs, in spite of the Kirlians."

"But Corman knew I was after him long enough in advance to substitute a humanoid for his evening walk. How sharp can you get? He must know who I am."

"That doesn't follow—think about it."

"Think how?"

"He's one of a handful of top Techs—the kind you've gone after. And so he sent a humanoid to walk his usual exercise route. He expected, perhaps, that somebody would jump the robot. But he wouldn't necessarily know who that somebody was.''

The reasoning seemed to make instant sense. The young man—Chip—lost his scowl. He nodded. ''But,'' he argued, ''it still could be that the group— if it's more than one—that is suspicious enough to do such a thing, may also have these attacks I've been making connected with the return of the fleet to the solar system.''

''Look, Hal put you up to this. And he wasn't even along. Besides, let's not worry about one, or even a dozen suspicious Tech A's like Corman. If we have to, we'll take care of him, and them, later.''

''Maybe,'' said Chip, darkly, ''we should drive to his house, and catch him there. In the rush I left my syringe.''

''Don't worry about it, I said.''

The alien listener noted that the words about the space fleet were spoken casually. And he was relieved again, as he already had been many times by other conversations of the past few days.

There seemed to be no doubt. Not even these dissidents suspected the truth. The fleet had returned with a report of having defeated the aliens.

So we did the right thing, thought the alien, in programming every single human being aboard to believe that there had been a victory; and then sending the fleet home.

It was not always possible to know how to deal with a different intelligent species. Further study would be needed before the grim game of planet extermination began in earnest.

TWO

IT WAS A VERY large city; that was already obvious to the alien. But he still had no definite data of exactly how big. The matter of size had simply not come up in the overheard conversations.

A city operated by computers was the picture that seemed to come through. Operated—how? That was not obvious either.

The two men—the youth, Chip, and his older companion, Hank—drove along one quiet, residential street and then another, and then onto and along a brilliantly lighted thoroughfare lined by shops, most of which were still open.

People were everywhere—shoppers and shopkeepers, theatergoers and theater operators, strollers, cars like Hank's, a public bus moving along with, of all things, one of the passengers acting as driver. As Hank followed the bus, waiting for an opportunity to pass, first one, and then another passenger, took over the driving of the bus. Even more puzzling, some of the people who came aboard put money into the cash receiving box, and about an equal number did not.

A few moments later, these odd actions unexplained, Hank maneuvered past the bus; and they saw it no more. The car presently turned up a side street, which turned out to be a better class residential area, consisting of two-story houses. Into and up the driveway of one of these Hank guided the vehicle.

He drove through partial darkness into the lighted yard at the rear of the house. Two other cars were parked there. As Hank pulled over, intending to place his machine beside the others, they passed two youths. The two were chatting vehemently, and gesticulating as they did so. They were on Chip's side of the car; so he leaned out and called, "Hi, Walt! Hi, Don!" There was no response. The young men did not seem to be aware that they had been spoken to.

Hank said, "I see the boys are still re-fightin' the war."

"Yeah. Do it myself," replied Chip.

"You do it different," said Hank, in a significant tone.

"How do you mean?" Surprised.

"Think about it. They're harmless. You're not."

"Oh!" The goodlooking face scowled for a moment. Then: "Yeah. I see what you mean."

Hank turned off the motor, and said in a low voice, "Straighten your clothes! You look messed up."

The older man pushed his door open, and climbed out. Standing up in the shadow, he was revealed to be a stocky, medium-sized individual. He watched patiently as Chip slid over and used the rearview mirror to straighten his hair and his coat.

By the time Chip got out of the car, he looked—in the half-light—again like an overgrown but well-groomed teenager. He stepped past Hank and walked over to the two youths, who were still vigorously continuing their discussion. The first words that came through had a beginning sound to them. As if what must have been going on and on, was not at all at some middle. Don, the dark-haired one, said, "Boy, was that first drop to the surface scary! All those clouds, and not knowing what the aliens would do. And so cold—"

And the second youth—Walt—accepted the meaning as if it had . . . meaning. And added his nothing: "Yeah, you're not kiddin'! You'd think with a big blue sun like they got, the planet'd be tropical from top to bottom!"

Don babbled *his* emotion to that: "When I first saw that ice, far as the horizon, I yelled at my sarge, 'Hey, these stupes are landing us at the north pole!' "

And then Walt: "Nobody said nothin' to that; so you can bet the officers were as shook-up as the rest of us. . . ."

Both young men seemed to be momentarily silenced by their memories. So Chip interjected hastily: "Hey, you guys, come up to my room in a little."

As he turned away, he heard Don come to verbal life again. "And it *was* the north pole, for Pete's sake—"

At that point, Chip, following Hank, entered the house by the rear entrance; and the mad voice was chopped off by the door closing behind him.

Patiently, the alien watched the unfolding scene inside. A rather long hallway, dimly lighted. A second door. And then there was another, more brightly lighted hallway and a staircase. Several doors led off from this front hallway. A bright light poured forth from one of the doorways.

The two human beings, first the older—rapidly—

and then the younger one, dawdling, started up to the second floor.

Chip had gone only three steps when a woman's voice called from somewhere beyond the door through which the bright light came: "Is that you, Chip?"

Chip sighed, instantly impatient. "Yeah, sis."

"You all right?"

The youth made a face up at Hank, who had paused and turned. He said, "Yeah, for Pete's sake, of course. What else?"

"All right, all right, don't get mad!"

"I hate stupid questions."

"True feeling, true concern is never stupid."

Chip sighed again, and slumped a little. "Okay, forget it. I'm too bored to be mad. . . ." As he spoke, he took several more steps.

The alien thought that Chip and his sister were like the two automatons in the yard—compelled by an inner need to respond. On this level, noted the alien, this life form cannot really think. Bare instants later, his analysis was proved to be at least partially correct. The woman's voice yelled, "If your own sister hasn't got the right to be worried about you, who has?"

It could have ended there. But it was evident that the young man had a need to interact with his sister, and on a hostile basis; for he yelled back, "Look, baby, where I was for nearly four years, you should have worried. But you don't look like you did."

"I was plenty worried every minute you were out there in space."

"You don't look like you worried. You got married. You got heavier from eating the good things. So stop asking how I am. I hate phonies."

"I'm not a phony. I was worried every minute. The doctor says I overate to compensate."

"Listen, Dodie, your worry and what I was in, don't match. So cut it, will you?

Hank had paused at the top of the stairway. He stood there with a Good-God-how-long-will-this-go-on expression on his face. But the youth's final remarks seemed to have done their job; for the woman's voice was silent.

Chip, continuing up the staircase, suddenly seemed to think of something; for he paused, and called, "Anybody phone while I was out?"

The reply was subdued, "Yes, the phone numbers are in your room. And there was also a call for Hank. I put the message on his bed."

"Okay, thanks."

After that, the two men went all the way up. Hank turned right to a door only a few feet from the stairs. Chip continued on down the hall and opened a second door into the large bedroom above the living room below.

For the alien, it was an ideal location. In utilizing a portion of Chip's neural-spinal-brain network as his communication link with earth, the Ig had noticed an extended perception ability, of which the human being was unaware. The perceptions involved—sight and sound—came into the receiving center of the brain as pure signals. But were then subjected to a steady barrage of confusing associations.

The consequent incredible confusion made mind-reading impossible. But the equipment was there, available. The alien turned into the perceiving center, and manipulated the special ability for his own purposes.

At the moment, he simply allowed the extended awareness to sink through the floor, and into the living room below. It was the room from which Chip's sister, Dodie, had done all her yelling a minute earlier.

She was still there, sitting now with a book face down on her rather large lap. Across the room from her, also sitting, was Dodie's husband, John Scheim. John was a serious-faced individual of about thirty; and he had evidently been reading a paper; and had also—evidently—just lowered it to his lap. He said, "I really shouldn't let him talk to you like that."

The plump young woman was instantly on the defensive. "Now, John, take it easy. Chip is having a hard time settling down."

John said, "A husband, Dodie, should protect his wife from the kind of insults you just got, even though they did come from your own brother."

"He's been home only four days," the woman pointed out. "He's still on edge."

Her husband rubbed his chin, said, "When he phoned you, asked if he could bring along his buddy, did you have a picture of a bum like Hank, fifteen years older?"

The young woman was reluctant but honest. "No, I have to admit I thought it'd be another fellow like Chip, about twenty."

"We've got to notice once more, on the basis of the conversation you just had with your loving brother," said the man, "that human nature seems to come out of some hidden well of psychic poison. The wise men keep trying to locate the source of that negative madness. The old-time anarchists believed that, given the chance, men and women would turn into pure souls. Now that we've had anarchism for nearly a hundred years, those poor nuts are probably writhing in their graves with shame."

"But it's still the best system," said Dodie quickly.

"Without the Kirlians," said her husband flatly, "the place would tear itself apart in 3 hours."

John shrugged, and said in a tone that was more wry than angry, "Anyway, here we are, two of our three spare bedrooms taken up, and our food bill has already doubled. Have Chip or Hank made any contribution to the budget?"

"Not yet." The reluctant tone was back in her voice.

John said, "The private corporations that maintain the fleet paid each returnee $4,000, just like they did when I came back from our first tangle with the aliens. So both these guys have got plenty of cash."

"I suppose Chip thinks it's all right to sponge off his sister."

Her husband quoted, " 'Justice requires that every adult human shall have a fair share of the goods of the world, and that no one shall be deprived of life or liberty by his own, or someone else's, out-of-control motivations to do violence in any of its numerous forms.' And," he added, "that surely includes that everyone shall pay his own way, and nobody take advantage of another."

"I promise," said Dodie, "when they've sponged for one week, I'll speak to Chip."

The man nodded. "I'll buy that."

"Thank you, dear."

He sighed, and said, resignedly, "I suppose a gang will soon be trooping over here, and they'll all spend the night drinking and yelling at each other, and playing that loud music."

"Our bedroom," argued the overweight young woman, "is downstairs and out of the way; so we won't really be disturbed. The place is big enough."

"I can hear them," said her husband. "Maybe you can't."

Dodie said in a hopeful voice, "One of the messages—the one for Hank—was from that man, Hal somebody. Maybe they'll all go over there like they did the first night."

John said, "I'm not complaining very hard yet. But the constant jabber of some of those characters—ugh!"

The woman did a shudder. "It must have been awful, fighting those aliens. They've all got to have time to get it out of their systems."

"What I'd like to have," said the man, darkly, "is some kind of a coherent story about what happened out there in space. Everything seems to have been too easy. After all, I was there ten years ago; and that time we didn't even get to land."

"There's one good thing about your having been there, too," said his wife. "At least, Chip will have to respect you for that."

"I don't think he respects anybody yet," said her husband.

For the alien, the scene had suddenly dimmed, and the voice of the man seemed far away. The instant implication was, of course, that Chip had left the bedroom upstairs, and was going farther away each passing moment. The objective evidence for that came moments later, as Dodie said hastily, "They're coming downstairs, and they seem to be in a hurry."

That was a truth which the alien was able to verify as he manipulated himself back to Chip, and found him charging down the stairs, followed at the same three-steps-at-a-time pace by Hank.

The two men raced out of the same back door by which they had entered the house minutes earlier, and headed toward Hank's car. *En route* they obviously saw that there had been some new arrivals— another car from which a young black and a young red-headed white were emerging.

To these, and to the two obsessive historians, Don and Walt, Chip yelled, "Hal says somebody's trying to take over the fleet. We've got to get back up there, and see what's going on."

THREE

THE WATCHER WAS baffled at this totally unexpected development. Rescue the fleet! The alien contemplated the improbability of any one, or two, or three—or as many hundreds, for that matter—persons undertaking such a mission.

In the central Ig confederation, the armed vessels were controlled by an agreement among about a score of planetary governments. The agreement involved the lateran unity, which of course human beings could never have.

The alien drew a blank as he tried to imagine how else the massive firepower of a fleet could be rationally dealt with. . . . He could only wait and see what developed.

His referent on earth—the youth named Chip—was again in Hank's car. And so there they were driving, as before, through the night at about thirty miles per hour. The direction they were going was different. Also, this time, there were four men in the car: Hank and Chip in the front seat; the black youth and the freckle-faced country type in the back—these were the two young men that had arrived just as Chip and Hank came hurrying out of the Scheim house.

During the entire hasty departure, the other two

youths—Don and Walt—had not even looked up from their absorption with each other's reminiscences.

Four male human beings, three of them quite young; but all four seeming to accept the validity of what they were doing.

It was the black who broke the silence—and the illusion of an agreement. He pursed his lips into a scowl, and said, "What's this rescue-the-fleet thing?"

The husky youth in the front seat shrugged. "Hank got a message, Mike. So we're heading to see what the story is."

The slender young black leaned back in his seat, crossed his legs in a relaxed manner, and said, "What do we care who controls the fleet? If somebody wants to take on all that responsibility, for God's sake let 'em!"

There was a distinct pause—which the alien welcomed. . . . For God's sake, he thought—using the same expletive, mentally—what kind of an idea is that? Let anyone have the fleet who wants it!

He grew aware that Chip was frowning. The question and the comment seemed to have made an impression on him. He glanced at Hank, then looked away, twisting his mouth in puzzlement, then looked at Hank again. And this time said, "A couple of days ago, Hank, we were all relieved to get off those ships, and let the maintenance robots take over. Now, suddenly, Hal—who wasn't even along on our four-year nightmare—sounds the alarm; and, boy, we're off to do or die. What about it, Hank?"

The tone was condemnatory; but if Hank was aware he did not let it disturb him. He continued to watch the night street ahead, and said in an even voice, "Just trust Hal, Chip. He's the smartest guy I ever met. And if he says there's a problem, it's so. But, most important for you, remember your special situation. Also, Hal was on that expedition that came back ten years ago; and so he's got a background in all this."

From the rear seat, Mike said in his most indolent tone, "There's three good men and true in this vehicle, *plus* Hank." He waved vaguely in the direction of the roof of the car. "Up there are fifteen big ships in orbit. Which one are we headin' toward, hey? Or maybe we'll have time to visit two before breakfast—if we can stay awake."

Chip said, "I'll let the insulted man answer that." He grinned at Hank.

The car continued along as before, with the people inside it silent. Presumably, the three youths were waiting for Hank to react, and presumably Hank was considering what his reaction should be.

Abruptly, he seemed to decide. He said, "I'm handicapped in this. I think Mike does mean well by Chip, but he's too young to know what's good for anybody. Hal and I are the best things that ever happened along for Chip, the way he is right now. So I don't regard what Mike said as an insult. He doesn't understand life, at his age."

Chip's grin had broadened, as the explanation proceeded. Now, he turned to Mike. "Okay, boy," he said, "you got an earful of the kind of insult that you can take your time answering. I guess I'd better answer your question." He shrugged. "Only one ship up there Hank and I care about—the one that's got all the anti-Kirlian stuff tuned to me."

Mike's reaction was grim. His eyes narrowed. "I got a bunch of thoughts about that," he said, "but I won't say none of them right now. However, since I'm your best pal and got your best interests at heart, I'll get around to it before morning. You won't like what I have to say."

At the wheel, Hank wiggled, frowned, licked his lips. "I'm Chip's best pal," he protested. "And *I* got his best interests at heart."

The freckle-faced youth in the rear seat next to Mike did a body twisting movement of his own. He said, "I came along because Mike said Chip has got to be rescued from Hal and Hank; and by God that's what I'm here for." Mike rolled his great brown eyes. "What I like about these bright boys like Dave here is the way they open those big fat yaps and put in both feet.

Chip was scowling. "What's this stuff about rescuing me from one of my best friends, Mike?"

"Yeah," said Hank, without turning, "what am I supposed to be doing to him?"

Mike waved a black, dismissing hand. "We'll talk about this at breakfast—which is a long way off. Right now, I see we're coming to the take-off pad, where the shuttles used to be. And—" He pressed his cheek against the closed window on his side, and peered out into the darkness to the right, "and where it looks like most of 'em still are. . . ."

He leaned back, with a shrug. "So it's not a big fleet takeover yet. Chip, you sure you want to do this?"

Even as he asked the question Hank was pulling over to the curb, where it was quite dark. They all climbed out into a world of shadows and night, and in single file walked across the sidewalk and onto the special paved section; actually a very complex substance with which an anti-gravity drive could interact.

As they walked through the darkness Chip said, "Come on, Mike, what bothers you about Hank?"

Mike was silent for a moment and then said, "You two have a most peculiar association. An old man of thirty-five takes an interest in an overgrown kid of twenty, and helps him use the great power of a war vessel to counteract what makes today's civilization possible—meaning the Kirlian computers. Now, we had to have that kind of control of the Kirlian thing out in space—but there's no record of anyone before Hank ever doing what he's done for Chip. And, moreover, I still can't figure why you let it be done, Chip."

For more than a minute as the dialogue proceeded, the alien had been torn between two purposes. On the one hand, he wanted to hear the interchange—it seemed suddenly very significant. On the other hand, he was striving to perceive the darkness ahead; particularly, he wanted to establish how the place was protected.

What was startling, and distracting, was that he couldn't see anyone or anything. No guards. No human supervision. No barriers. No lights. What his perception brought back to him was that there was nobody on the launch pad, with its hundreds of shuttles, with the power to restrict use of the marvellous equipment.

The intruders seemed totally unaware that there was anything unusual in their surroundings. The three youths and Hank continued to move along in and out, turning now this way and now that. The four seemed to be heading toward some specific destination.

And, in fact, suddenly, a light glared in Hank's fingers. The thin, bright beam flickered over the dully gleaming surface of, first, one and then a second, and finally a third shuttle. At which point Hank said, "Here we are, number 86A431." They walked deliberately under the overhanging shuttle up to the circular structure which supported it. It was the shuttle that, moments before, he had identified as apparently the one they wanted.

The round, supporting structure was about eight feet high and twenty feet in diameter. Surmounting it like a toadstool or a mushroom on its stem—the circular, supporting structure being the stem—was the shuttle.

Hank reached forward gingerly with an outstretched finger, and did something. Either touched a *nis* (neural interact surface), or pressed a button. Whatever it was, a door slid open and a light turned on revealing an up staircase.

For the three youths, it was the equivalent of old home week. They trotted forward and bounded up two stairs at a time. When they had gone past him, Hank followed them. As he started up the steps, an automatic process closed the sliding door.

The rapidly receding body of Chip put a pressure on the Ig. But he resisted and took one final look, while he held his perception outside the shuttle. The night scene here on this remote (from Ig) planet, earth, had an eerie quality. Seeing the dimly visible row on row of toadstool shapes satisfied what he believed to be a deep, artistic sensitivity.

We really are the great ones, he thought finally. Our game of endless conquest is taking us to these distant alien lands. And the game brings much pleasure. . . .

With that satisfying realization, he permitted his perception to drift upward. Moments after that he was once more at a comfortable distance from his host nervous system. Close to Chip. Inside the shuttle.

Surprisingly, it was a slightly more exciting experience than he had anticipated. Nothing to do with the interior of the shuttle, itself. He had presumed that it was the same craft that had brought Chip and the others down to earth a few days ago. And so far as he could see it was.

The same cramped quarters, mostly taken up with seats for passengers. The three youths, in fact, were already sitting in the comfortable red passenger chairs near the stairs. And Hank, the technician, had settled into the equally comfortable black chair in front of the small control panel.

That part was familiar, normal, unexciting. Equally ordinary was the panel itself. The lights were on, and shifting color. Indicating that power was building up systematically. At any instant, now, the gravity interaction between the ship and the·pad material below would come to its zero point. And then go minus.

The lift began quietly. The shuttle floated up like a cork in a tub that was rapidly filling with water, bobbing a little but otherwise stable. Except, of course, that this "tub" was the size of a planetary atmosphere. And the celestial "faucet" that was filling it was pouring in the equivalent of oceans every minute.

And so as the power continued to build, the gravity-minus effect increased geometrically. Faster and faster the shuttle bobbed upward. The Ig acknowledged that it was a good system. It lacked principally the maching-living organism interface, which the Ig had by way of their lateran unity. And, of course, these poor, unsuspecting would-be defenders of the fleet had no awareness of the extended perception by which their surroundings could have been visible and audible to them. That was what was now, suddenly, exciting.

In floating up from the ground, the Ig-Chip extended perception had passed through the shuttle's luggage compartment. Obviously, Chip and his friends had not paused to glance into those dark spaces. It was obvious because if they had, and turned on a light or two, they would have seen instantly that a dozen men were hiding in it.

Apparently, the fleet takeover started right here in the shuttle.

And the four intrepid rescuers had—equally apparently—not noticed.

FOUR

AS SUCH THINGS often are, the way of the confrontation was simple—and direct.

Time edged forward. The shuttle soared. The darkness outside transformed from an atmospheric dimness to a black night filled with what looked like individual bits of bright powdered snow.

As the small universe in and around one planet of a single sun system thus manifested, the seemingly magical performance of in-phase machinery began.

From out of the night of space flashed a ship. At least, that was the appearance of what happened. The great vessel, which was one unit of the earth fleet, *seemed* to come toward the shuttle at a darting speed. As if it would fly by at some colossal velocity and disappear into remoteness.

Not quite like that. The fleet ship was actually in a fixed orbit, always over the same spot far below. The other ships of the fleet were similarly in fixed spots over other exact surface areas. What was below was invariably a launch pad, like the one from which Shuttle Number 86A431 had come.

Enormous speeds *were* involved, but it was in-phase rendezvous. Perfect approach. Activation of the big ship's airlock mechanism at exactly the right instant. The shuttle glided forward, and slid in along a track. When it was completely inside, its passage triggered a relay that closed the outer door silently behind it. As the shuttle came to rest, another relay started a flow of air back into the interior of the airlock. Whereupon Hank manipulated the shuttle door; and he and Chip and Mike and Dave went down the stairs and into the ship.

At which point the concealed ones emerged in single file from the baggage compartment, and came down the steps behind them, and so into the inside of the spaceship.

And there they all suddenly were together.

Dave showed fear; he cringed. Chip's eyes narrowed thoughtfully. His gaze darted over the faces of the newly arrived men, and he seemed to be searching for something in each face. Hank backed over against a metal wall, and showed his teeth.

Mike stayed where he was, and it was he who spoke the first words. "Hey!" he said. "We're outnumbered." His brown eyes widened and brightened. "Chip, what do you think? Groups of twelve guys each are taking over the fleet. Twelve is a precise number. Maybe that many waited on every shuttle, waiting to grab whoever came aboard. Hal conned us into a trap."

There was a protesting sound from Hank. But it was an inarticulate thing; a noise and not a word.

No one else said anything immediately. Every face was tense in some way. The twelve were all grown men, thirty or over. It was apparent from the expressions on the faces of Chip, and Hank, and Dave, and Mike that they did not recognize any of the intruders.

It was almost as quickly obvious that at least two of the twelve recognized Chip. One of the two was black-haired, grim, but smiling in a twisted way. He said into a tiny wrist radio: "We've got him!"

The second man was equally grim, but there was no smile on his face. He had brown hair and long, brown sideburns; and he also spoke into a wrist radio, saying crisply: "The rest of you go home. We'll handle this S.O.B."

Both men had their eyes pointed at Chip as they spoke.

Mike visibly did a doubletake on that, and then said softly, "Hey, Chip, you're the target of this fleet takeover."

Presumably, thought the remote alien watcher, whose awareness "floated" near Chip . . . presumably, Chip with his mental control of the great vessel's Kirlian computers can dominate this situation.

Exactly what he did with his "control" would provide priceless information. And if he couldn't dominate, the details of *that* should be equally interesting.

Chip and his friends did a swift lookaround. In that flicking of eyes this way, that way, they visibly evaluated their location.

It was not good.

They were in a large assembly room. From where they stood at the rear of the place, they could look over long rows of seats, which faced away from them. It was like a theater, except that the seats were unusually well cushioned. And so was the floor. And the ceiling. And the walls. Also, each chair had an elaborate seat belt, and not a single hard or pointed edge anywhere. This was where the crew could hastily, on signal, strap themselves in for rapid acceleration.

Three aisles provided access to the seats and passage to the far side—front—of the room. And what was unfortunate was that the group of twelve adversaries had, as individuals, taken up positions barring all routes including the one back to the shuttle.

It was a moment when leadership qualities revealed themselves. On Chip's face, a decision took form. He glanced around. "Well, gentlemen," he said courteously, "if you will step out of the way my party and I wish to depart back for earth."

Nobody moved. In fact, the two men in front of the shuttle entrance actually seemed to brace themselves.

Chip looked over at Hank. His gaze met narrowed eyes. The youth's own face held a twisted smile. He said lightly, "Looks like a bunch of stupes, eh, Hank?"

Hank said tensely, "Getting any Kirlian feedback, Chip?"

"I haven't tried anything. It takes a ritual."

"I suspect this is the Kirlian Responsibility Group," said Hank, "with both Tech unions equally represented."

"Good lord!" said Chip, disgustedly.

"In which case," continued Hank, "they can probably, working together, counteract anything you can do."

"Well," Chip sighed, "we might as well find out what they plan to do. I—"

That was as far as he got. A large, blond man had been reacting to Hank's and Chip's interchange. From one pocket he drew a gleaming instrument. Then he said, "By God, enough of this!" Simultaneously, something bright discharged from the instrument and flashed over and into Chip high on the right shoulder.

It was the same kind of harmful light the robot had used a few hours before. Chip's response was similar to what it had been then. He uttered a cry of pain, and staggered.

The weapon had been discharged from behind and one side of Chip and his companions. So it was not clear immediately what had happened. Thus it was that two others of the group of twelve darted forward. They grabbed Chip and held him.

No one else moved.

Mike seemed to be the first to realize that something adverse had occurred. He said, anxiously, "Hey, Chip, you all right?"

Chip was still partly held up; but he was also partly holding himself. And so, though he said nothing, it was obvious that he still had some of his wits in gear.

The big blond man who had "fired" the weapon, spoke again. "Well, fellows," he addressed his companions, "what do we do? Right now, for us, this is a control-free area. We could shoot him; and that part of the problem is over."

Chip came to. And he must have heard the meaning. Though still held, he straightened, and said softly, "Hear that, Hank? Tech A attitudes." He shook his head, chidingly. "These capitalist types!"

"You're one yourself."

"I chose the lesser of two evils, but I have to admit it's pretty sickening sometimes."

"Maybe you're lucky there are some Tech B's here."

Chip seemed not to hear. He said softly, "To a capitalist type, other people are not real. He or she is not real to we. We are not real to he or she. It's a two-way blankness by which we tolerate pain, damage, or death for he or she. But if that same damage is done to we, suddenly outrage, suddenly a requirement of 'fair' treatment for me. We capitalists learned a reluctant lesson long ago. In order to get fair treatment for ourselves we must, as a group, require it for others, also. Thus, reason, not feeling, produced a system called justice, whereby guilt is adjudicated, and harm is done to the guilty party by the group. All this, also, had to go, because, of course, people are not guilty, period." He glanced at the blond man, grinned, and said, "I'm not guilty, sir."

Toward the end of Chip's monologue, the big man started to walk toward him, as if he, also, had something to say. As he came up, without more than a twitch of warning he struck Chip a terrific blow across the face.

"Wipe that goddamn smile off your face!" he said savagely.

The blow had so much force that the blond youth was flung back against the two men who were holding him. He fell so hard that they were thrown off balance, also. They staggered back and around yet stubbornly continued to hold onto Chip. It looked as if all three of them would go down.

But they managed. They recovered. Then one of them snarled, "Bracely, if you interfere with our prisoner again, I'll break your arm."

Bracely was apologetic. "You Tech B's are too soft with rats like this, but alright."

Chip seemed to accept that as a result of the interchange he was again protected. He glanced over at Mike. "We just had a fast look at basic human nature. Pretty evil, eh?"

"Chip, shut up!" admonished Mike, uneasily. "You're in trouble, and maybe you deserve it."

Incredibly, Chip grinned. "That," he said, "removes you from the status of being my best pal, and puts Hank back into first place."

Whereupon, he and Hank exchanged a significant glance—which the Ig observed, and could not interpret.

I, analyzed the alien, have been with this young human from the instant that he emerged from the memory-changing process. During that time I have heard everything that he has said, seen what he has seen, been with him every moment that he was in the presence of another human being—"

There was nothing Chip could possibly have kept secret. No action, no thought communicated that the Ig had not noticed. And yet—now, suddenly, it was as if a message passed between Hank and Chip. Something completely understood by both of them, but remaining unspoken.

Could it be—was it possible—that these two knew the truth?

The alien had no time to consider the improbability of that. Because the men were turning, moving.

Bracely said, "Bring that young rat along. It's time we got him over to the computer room, and disconnected him for good."

Chip must have deduced that he was the "rat" referred to; for he taunted, "What about shooting me?"

The big man had started off ahead. At Chip's words, he turned. He said grimly, "Derner, you shut that guy up, or I'll let him have it again."

It was not obvious which of the two men leading Chip was Derner. They both wore suits and were about equal height—five feet ten—and both physically sturdy. One of the two was in his late twenties and the other in his middle thirties. The slightly older of these two said to Chip, "Listen, kid, slow down! You're not in a position to carry on an equal dialogue. Start walking!"

Chip walked jauntily. In a more subdued fashion after him came Mike and Hank and Dave. All dozen of their captors infiltrated around them, in front, to the side and behind. They used one of the aisles to get to the far side of the assembly room. There they entered a corridor and a few moments later stepped onto a rapidly moving conveyor belt.

It was as they were whisking along that Hank turned to the man behind him and said in a cajoling voice, "What's this all about, fellow?"

"It's the old military story," was the reply. "Out there in space these military types get the feel of power. Their egos soar. When they come back here, with the usual military mind justification they start to figure out how they can keep their power." The speaker sighed. "It's a sad thing to realize that human nature keeps repeating the same old patterns."

As if overwhelmed by the argument, Hank's mouth had fallen slightly open.

The man went on: "Not satisfied with the victory out there over the aliens, these military types scheme to overthrow our perfect political system. They just can't stand to see people who are not subject to their orders."

"So," persisted Hank, "why does that rate rough treatment for my friend Chip?"

"He's been back four days, and he's already beat up on seven people. Naturally, we figured right away it must be a returned man who, somehow was still connected to a ship computer. So we put a directional trace on the fleet computer use of the past few days. It was a different computer each time; so we figure he may be connected to all fifteen of 'em."

"And what," asked Hank in a strained voice, "are you going to do?"

"We're going to disconnect him and turn him loose. That's the majority decision." The man added, "A minority wanted to kill him, but we decided even military types should get equal benefit."

They had come to the end of the conveyor belt, and were stepping off gingerly onto another padded corridor floor. Chip must have heard the explanation; for he turned his head, and said, "I like the being turned loose part; so like a, uh, good soldier, I'll hold still for the disconnection."

They walked through a door into—dimness. A large room lighted by a faint ceiling glow, here and there, a floor with an occasional shining square, and a few radiant spots on each of three walls. The brightness from these penetrated but did not entirely disperse an overall effect of twilight.

After a little, after their eyes grew accustomed, there came into focus a long line of metal poles. They were like pillars, thirty of them altogether, evenly spaced at a distance from each other of about three feet. All thirty of them were lined up in front of the wall opposite the door, the wall which gave off no light.

The pillars made up the computer center of this giant ship.

The entire huge vessel was, of course, dotted with what the Techs called operating Kirlians. Each of these subordinate units carried out the central programming, and each transmitted information back to central whenever it acted, describing what it had done.

But a subordinate could not have its programming altered.

In the early days before anybody realized the anarchistic potentialities, Kirlians were used as police aids. They helped guard buildings and other property. And they resisted invading armies so stubbornly that forces moving into cities were brought to a complete stop.

A unit knocked down by artillery fire would lie there, twisted, shattered, but still sputtering, still trying to do its programming; in short, a magnificent barrier until it was shot into total inactivity.

Here in the computer center of the ship the programming *could* be altered. And that, of course, was what was now done. A greatly subdued Chip silently, on being directed, lay down on a flat surface of the programming section. The electronic "eyes" from an equally flat surface above him thereupon examined his whole body, and over on the programming chair the big fellow —Bracely—said in an even voice: "This that you are noticing is Chip Mitchum. Cancel his status as an honorary Kirlian. Hereafter, from the moment that he sets foot again on the planet earth he is to be treated like any human being, fully responsible for all his actions."

It was pretty ridiculous that a human being could be so precisely differentiated from all other human beings by a machine. Equally outrageous that the machine could then be instructed to treat him like another machine—i.e. not as a human being. And thereafter *all* computers who "noticed" him would instantly have a feedback from one of the centrals, instructing it that this is "one of us," and is not subject to the usual penalties.

Pretty ridiculous—but that was what Hank, acting as Hal Steggars' agent, had done for Chip, and what Chip had allowed to be done for him.

Now, it was undone.

On the down journey Chip sat strapped into an aisle seat of the shuttle, silent and pale, now. Hank, sitting next to him, had a faraway look in his eyes. Only Mike and Dave were cheerful.

Dave said, "We got out of that better'n I expected."

Hank stirred, turned. "We didn't get out of it."

"Huh!"

"Chip has lost his ability to deal with the Kirlians."

"So?" That was Mike. "Puts him back with the rest of us."

"It isn't that simple.

"Okay, Chip," said the black youth, "what exactly have you lost?"

"Well," hedged Chip, "I have to admit, most of it was kind of dull. You can watch a small part of the world through the eye of a particular Kirlian. For example, what's going on in a particular street. What the Kirlian, of course, is watching for is the emotion of violence and a bunch of other lesser stuff. But it's like a camera trained on a tiny area. After an hour, the camera is still there. A year later, same street. The guy or women walking toward you even look like the same people."

"Probably are," chimed in Mike.

"What's powerful about it," continued Chip, "is that if you know what you want you can switch over to any Kirlian on the circuit, and you can look at the street it is watching. Each street, all by itself is dull, but the ability to look at any street that has a Kirlian on it—and they all do—is like a Tech extension of human perception. And, of course—" he finished— "as long as you're an honorary computer, the others won't zap you even if you kill somebody. Which, naturally, I never did. The problem is, I'm not protected anymore from what I did do."

"We're in trouble," said the man. He glanced at the youth beside him. "Chip, do you think I should call Hal and ask his opinion before you leave this shuttle?"

There was a long pause, and then slowly Chip lifted his sturdy body out of its slump. "I might as well find out," he mumbled, "what the nearest Kirlian does to me. If it shoots me, then call Hal."

He laughed curtly, and twisted about in his seat to look at Mike and David. "Gentlemen," he said in a bitter tone, "we have just witnessed the first step of a free society protecting itself from danger. And, boy, did they misread the signs, and, boy, did they ever mess it up!"

For the Slua-Ig, it was the moment. The words had, at last, and for the very first time, the sound of unthinkingness. On his faraway planet, the alien, recognizing what he had heard as being the giveaway statement, emitted the Ig variant of a sigh of relief.

He knows. Chip knows.

What was amazing was that one man—or, perhaps, two, if Hank were included—had managed not to reveal until now the most decisive survival information for the human race ever to be available in one lone brain. Or two.

The alien made his moves swiftly. First, he did the lateran connection with the Ig commander of the fleet which had followed the human expedition back to earth.

They became a lateran unity, two minds interflowing their knowledge in the way that had long ago made the Ig realize that they were the perfect life form.

Of course, their communication was *not quite* pure. They were, after all, members of a race that played games not only with other races but with each other.

And so, even as their two minds joined, the Slua-Ig automatically withheld his private thoughts, and pretended—that was Step One of *his* game—that he was being open and sincere, and without barriers. Presumably, the fleet commander was doing the same thing; although subordinates were forbidden to be gameplayers.

Outwardly *and* inwardly, the dialogue which now took place seemed to be free of any and all mental reservations—which, naturally, was the ideal game condition.

Within the perception and sensory frame of the lateran unity, the player asked, ''When can the fleet begin its conquest of earth?" The commander answered that the vessels were of course no longer in the the distance-spanning state. The fleet was in a coasting orbit one point 0 one 02 time periods from earth at solar speeds.

Having become familiar with earth time, the great Ig translated that. It came to 14¼ earth days.

"The problem that remains," said the commander, "is the defense these people put up against us when we originally made our attack. That mustn't be allowed to happen again."

The gameplayer did the equivalent of a superior smile. He reminded the fleet officer that when the earth ships had been captured, it had been discovered that the Kirlians aboard supervised voting procedure, whereby the men elected their officers every three months, and then provided penalties if the men disobeyed their elected leaders. Naturally, the officers seldom gave orders because they wished to be re-elected.

"As you may recall," he said, "the consequent lax discipline is what enabled us to capture the entire expedition, hypnotically indoctrinate them, and release them."

"It did seem to be an unusually easy capture for us," acknowledged the military chieftain.

"Now, on earth," continued the Slua-Ig, "the Kirlians are programmed differently."

As he explained it, on each ship there was an in-depth Kirlian system, whereby a thousand outlets watched and observed every corridor and every room. Each outlet was a complete, self-sustaining computer. None of the thousand or so outlets *needed* the others to function, but they nevertheless were all interconnected and all set to do the same job. So much was this so that when one did something in the line of Kirlian duty, the others immediately added the action to their store of information. And it was something they thereafter took into account, almost as if they had done it themselves; except of course that they all "knew" the location of the originating unit.

On the planet itself the same interconnection occurred among billions of units. "They're as common as street lamps; and what Chip is now afraid of is that one of these units will react to his past misdeeds."

When this happened—boasted the gameplayer—every nuance of the earthside Kirlian response would be analyzed, and exact control methods worked out for both the youth and the computers.

He continued in the same satisfied way, "Some time before the fleet arrives I have one final investigation to make. A man named Hal Steggars. Without arousing suspicion I want Chip to visit this Hal."

Chip had already visited Hal once. "But," the gameplayer confessed, "I was not alert to Hal's possible importance, and did not take advantage of the opportunity. We'll be in touch."

"You're sure you'll be able to control such a complex system from Ig?" The commander sounded doubtful. "We out here want to win—and go home."

"The programming is actually very one-channeled. It's aimed at the emotion associated with the impulse to do violence. May I disconnect?"

The commander allowed the lateran effect to dissolve.

At once, mentally, the Slua-Ig reviewed the conversation. He had to admit his admiration for the fleet officer's uncriticizable comments. Not a hint of thoughts withheld. Every communication apparently aboveboard. It was supreme gameplaying.

His own game with the commander was, of course, designed to put over the idea that—except for one or two minor confusions—he had completely solved the human complexity. That admission about Hal Steggars was a nice example of a small aspect of the problem still to be examined.

The unhappy truth was, he wanted the fleet on its way because there were already so many blank areas. The fact was that he had a strong feeling that this race ought to be destroyed quickly. His task, meanwhile, was to build up an acceptable game picture of human beings at work, at play, at politics. This was his first species-destroying game, and he had had the tough luck to get a race that did seemingly illogical things.

So his game had to be so skillful that the unfinished picture of the planet and its inhabitants that he presently filed with the Game Assignment Committee not only looked finished but made him, as a gameplayer, look perfect.

FIVE

IT WAS THE second day later.

On the bed Chip lay unconscious. Periodically, his sister tiptoed into the room and looked at him, then tiptoed out again.

The alien waited. Outside, it was another bright, sunny day. Twelve and a quarter more such days, and then the fleet would arrive. So there was still plenty of time to be patient. Time to let Chip's condition evolve through some natural sequence of events, and to discover what those events were.

What had already happened was clear enough. The young man had lost his mental control over the computers of the fleet warships. And so, two nights earlier as the shuttle landed and the door swung open, Chip walked tensely out onto the pad. A fog had rolled in and over everything there was now a murky mist. Slowly, Chip moved forward into that mist, past three shuttles—and then abruptly he went limp.

For the alien it was a moment of triumph. For he spotted exactly where the computer was that had . . . reacted . . . against the youth. Instantly, his perception was over at the post—that was what it seemed to be, a tall metal post. The slender object poked up from some depth of the pad material. It pretended to be one of a line of guide posts, which normally signalled descending shuttles and helped them come down into their proper location.

What he had discovered was that a beam of coherent light was directed at Chip, penetrated his skin, chemically affected his blood stream, anaesthesizing him. And here he now lay.

Interesting. And educational.

Chip opened his eyes exactly on schedule, as deduced in advance from the type of anaesthetic created by the laser. For a while he simply experienced wakefulness. Awareness of the bed under him. Visualization of the ceiling above. Recognition that this was his room in his sister's house. The sense of having slept, and slept.

He yawned finally. And realized that an odor of food was coming in through the door. He parted his lips, and said, "Hey, everybody!"

His voice sounded exceptionally small in his ears. And the sound of it seemed to echo hollowly. It reminded him of something. A memory came. And realization.

Oh, my God, he thought, I'm down here now with the rest of the human race. Trapped as they are trapped. The shock made him draw his knees up against his stomach.

Time passed. The shock faded. Chip lay on his back and gazed ruefully up at the ceiling. . . . So that's the end of that, he thought ruefully. The end of his advantage over the computer.

The extent of his defeat was awesome to contemplate. For it had taken endless scheming and considerable technical skill to maintain a wartime and mind-machine interface in the hope that it would be useful against the otherwise overwhelming science of the alien enemy.

What can I do now? he wondered. That was the

first question. The second question was: How much time do I have?

There was an error in both questions. Both presupposed that he had free will. And he didn't. The Ig watcher looked down at the solved body of Chip Mitchum, and was pleased with the total—completely total—control that he had worked out for that body in the course of two days. By careful manipulation he could adjust the youth's nervous system in relation to a Kirlian computer. At his signal, the Kirlian reaction could take place *as if* Chip was in the act of committing violence.

Equally important, if Chip were in fact engaged in a vicious act, he could be skillfully manipulated so that the apparent emotion would be some relative of sweetness and light.

The great defenders of humankind were brought to subjugation in one easy lesson.

The expected ordinary things began to happen suddenly. The overweight sister came tiptoeing in again—and this time discovered the awakened younger brother.

Lots of emotion. Torrents of words. And time actually went by in sufficient quantity for afternoon to wane into twilight. But finally Chip was able to erect the old barrier of For-God's-sake-Sis-it's-not-the-end-of-the-world.

In a way that was true. The end was still twelve days away. And so the sisterly madness ran its course. Chip was lovingly fed, and urged to go back to sleep, and rest. The food he accepted. The advice he countered with a request that Hank be sent in.

They were really back to normal now. For after he had spoken the words about Hank, there was an unpleasant pause. Then Dodie said reluctantly, "Hank went out. He said something about going over to visit that man Hal."

"Oh—good!" The youth lay back in his bed, and seemed to relax for the first time.

There was a pause. Then the woman said, "Chip, John talked to one of the Kirlian people. You're going to have to change your way of life."

Lying there, Chip shrugged. His lean youthful face seemed to express the thought: So what else is new. Aloud, he said, "Okay."

"John wants to come in and talk to you this evening." His sister spoke anxiously. "Is it all right?"

He spread his hands, in an accepting way. "Got nothing else on, so far as I can see."

She went out; and after a while, after it was dark outside, her husband came in. He drew up a chair, and sat down in it, and said, "Everything has its good side. Your being knocked out like this gives me my first chance to talk to you."

Chip said, "I guess we vicious military types *are* kind of hard to communicate with."

John grinned. His face was actually quite good-looking when it smiled. A tendency to jowl disappeared at such moments. Still grinning he said, "I don't know what the Tech A union thinks, but a Tech B Kirlian Responsibility type talked to me."

The youth's face curled with contempt. "Those stupes!" he said. He shrugged. "Alright, tell me the sad story."

John's face indicated that he did not regard the remark as being very promising. He drew a deep breath, and said, "You ought to feel lucky that the

Co-op union is the one that's being allowed to settle your affairs."

Chip said, "About one Tech in every thousand has got a brain of his own. The rest, A or B, got nothing on their little minds but Tech rules, regulations, and rights."

"I thought you became quite a Tech yourself out there in space," said his brother-in-law.

"With me it's an avocation," shrugged the youth. "With a Tech it's a way of life."

"Then you don't regard your Tech training on those military ships as being the equivalent of an education?"

Chip could still be trapped. He suspected no ulterior motives in the question. "Hell, no!" he said.

"Still," said John Scheim, "you have to admit that on the whole they've handled their Kirlian responsibility without, as some people feared, taking advantage."

"I find it hard at this moment," said Chip, "to appreciate Techs Cap and Techs Co-op. Maybe they keep each other in line, but they're all the same kind of dummies to me."

"Okay." Resigned. "You ready?"

Chip's expression became consciously patient, but he said nothing.

The older man said, "You have to go to college—"

SIX

IT WAS Wednesday, August 30, 2102 A. D. The morning had been sunny, but now clouds hid that bulging, round, white hot, yellowish light source in earth's sky.

Hank, at the wheel, broke the silence first. "Just go through the motions," he said.

Chip, sitting in the front seat beside the older man, gestured in a way that had no obvious meaning to the observing alien. The gesture was with the thumb of his right hand. He made an "up" movement with it, then allowed the whole hand including the thumb to sink out of sight onto the seat beside him.

"Hal," continued Hank, "is checking his sources. The tip-off about the fleet takeover came from one of his most trusted men. As you know, it turned out to be a trap aimed specifically at you. So that guy is going to have to talk fast, to save himself."

Chip merely scowled. And the car now passed a sign with an arrow pointing ahead and the words: LOCAL UNIVERSITY 432. Hank pulled through the gate, stopped before a building labeled Administration, and said, "Mark time. Look as if you're sincere!"

"I presume you know what you're advising," said Chip.

"Yeah."

"What about a reaction from a Kirlian listening in on the interview?" said Chip.

Hank shrugged. "Don't give it a thought."

Chip said, "I got a feeling you were spoiled by the fleet Kirlians. There the first penalty was that the robot waiters wouldn't serve you food. You had to go to the refrigerators and find your own. Second penalty: certain refrigerator doors wouldn't open. Your choice of food was progressively restricted. But I have now had my first Kirlian-induced unconsciousness. I can tell you it's very convincing."

"You're not intending violence to anyone in the college, are you?"

"Of course not."

"Then what's the problem?"

"There are," said Chip, "harassments to which the Kirlians react in a lesser way. People who won't flush toilets, who pinch or slap, open other people's mail, violate another's privacy, never bathe, cheat at cards, make fun of someone else's religion, and— here's the one that applies indirectly to what you're recommending—people who spread misleading, or lying, or intent-to-harm-or-deceive gossip. I could get a dose of unconsciousness from ten minutes to several hours for any one of those."

"Only if you did them repeatedly," Hank dismissed.

"I'll take the bus home," said Chip, as he climbed out. And there was no doubt in what followed that their destination had registered in Chip's mind. For presently he was inside standing in a lineup in front of a window. Also, when it was his turn at the opening, Chip picked up the papers that were thrust toward him. However, at no time, in those first minutes, did he understand what he was supposed to do with what had been handed to him.

He had been following a red-haired youth and a black-haired girl, who were just ahead of him in the lineup. Now he went over and he sat down at a long table near them. The act of sitting down released him a little. Sitting required less of him, less energy, less concentration, less muscular effort. Thus he was able to frown down at the papers, to focus his eyes, and to think about what had happened to him.

Suddenly, then, he actually realized where he was. He felt vaguely ashamed of himself, as if he were a grown man, and here he was being treated like a teenager. Worse, still, he happened to glance at a mirror directly opposite his chair. The reflection that he stared at *was* of a teenager. Slightly overgrown, bulky in the shoulders, but a teen.

The awareness sobered him instantly. Briefly, some of the old sardonicism came back. "Get with it, boy!" he told himself. "What you need is an education. Can't get anywhere even in this perfect world without an education. And you didn't get one out there in space. All they taught you out there was to operate machinery until the stuff was coming out of your ears."

Thought of space brought a scowl and an impatience with himself. For the first time he examined the forms and saw that it was a simple routine. With that attitude, his practised eye ran over the questions. His fingers efficiently manipulated the pen, filling in the required details: name, address, military service if any, its nature, its length, his rank—

He sighed, and wrote, "lieutenant-colonel." He

suppressed an impulse to explain that where ninety-six percent of an expedition was made up, to start, of sixteen-year-olds, it didn't take long for somebody who took the whole thing seriously (as he had in the beginning) to be noticed and rewarded. So up there he had been elected into the higher ranks. Finally, when it was too late for the benefits of his straight life to be undone, he had got cynical. Fortunately, by that time even the older men were in a strange state of mind; so nobody noticed except Hank.

"Number forty-three!" said a voice once, then again.

There was a pause, then the youth next to Chip at the long table touched his arm, pointed at the card attached to the forms Chip had filled out, and said, "That's you."

A minute after that he was sitting at a desk facing a girl interviewer.

In the act of moving to his present position he had, unfortunately, got lost again. The sense of nothingness was back.

So he was not really conscious of the girl, except that she was one. As he leaned back, he had a vague impression of long golden hair dangling past an oval face, which was bent forward and down looking at the forms he had given her.

Presumably, what happened next could have been normal. She could have looked up and said a routine thing; and then he could have replied routinely. Like two automatons doing their job they could have gone through the entire process without ever making any more contact than two computers talking to each other impersonally.

But what she said was not routine. She looked up

with bright blue eyes and said, "Congratulations, Mr. Mitchum."

The question he anticipated was: "Are you Mr. Mitchum?" Chip's lips started to say,"yes, I'm Mitchum—" but didn't say that.

His eyes narrowed. He actually did a doubletake on the interview from beginning to now, scanning approximately one and three quarter minutes of time. The end result was the same. Her statement made absolutely no sense, it had no relation to anything he had written on the application. Her words had thrown him off guard. He said in a puzzled tone, "How do you mean, congratulations?"

"You made it." Her eyes were bright blue and shining. "You survived the trip."

Something about the meaning penetrated deep. An intense emotional darkness responded from that depth. "How does that get me congrats?"

"Somebody up there must like you," said the girl. She pointed hazily upwards.

The inner darkness engulfed him like a dark cloud. Chip said in a grim voice, "Listen, kid, stick to your business. I don't care for that remark."

He had a remote feeling that he was damaging his prospects; but a memory came of the destroyed spacecraft from which he was one of seventeen rescued personnel. And he couldn't stop. He rushed on, "Some of my best buddies are dead. You're saying that they're dead because somebody up there didn't like them. To hell with that."

If he had been his normal cool, studied self, Chip would have realized from the expression on the face across the desk from him, that he had overkilled. The oval pretty face was visibly stunned. "I beg your

50

pardon," the girl faltered. "I was just trying to say something nice."

Chip sneered, "You're probably one of these girls who's got bored with us up-tight vets. But you give us a sweet, understanding smile and try to make phony conversation."

She shook her head, numbly. "I've been crying ever since I first heard that three ships were lost. Each time I hear the details of how somebody got killed, I . . . oh, oh, here I go again."

She burst into tears.

The reaction was completely contrary to the scenario of her that he had so abruptly assembled in his mind. Chip was taken aback. "Hey, I'm sorry!" he said, anxiously.

"I can't help it," she sobbed. "It's so terribly sad."

The youth glanced around uneasily. "Okay, okay," he said, "you win. Look, get down to business. Everybody's staring at us. They'll be thinking I did something."

The girl began to write in a desperate fashion on the part of the first form where it said, "To be filled in by office staff." She was murmuring, "I'll be all right. It's not your fault. I shouldn't have said what I did. . . ."

Somewhere in there Chip realized that he was being handed a copy of his application, and being told that a board of admissions would pass on it, and that he would be advised. Also, as he walked out, he saw that she signed her name in the "office" part: Leslie Bjornson.

SEVEN

IT WAS STILL afternoon when he got outside, still cloudy. A breeze was blowing as Chip came out of the university grounds, and started to walk briskly along the street. Chip walked past the bus stop, turned up a side street, and came to a shopping center.

It all seemed very non-sequitur to the alien, whose attention was still back in the college, thinking about the interview. The question: what made Chip agree to go to college? There was something about this system that was still not clear.

Could the planet extermination game be considered played, if the system that was defeated were not properly understood? The question made him uneasy. He who had chosen to try to make minimum information appear maximum had better decide soon what that appearance should be.

The Slua-Ig felt an intense frustration . . . What was going on here? Chip was not threatening violence, the Kirlians were not involved. Chip had paused at the window of a clothing store. With pursed lips, he examined the items displayed there as if he were considering what was in the window in relation to some need of his own. The youth, apparently having made up his mind, headed for the entrance.

A sign just inside the door read: SELF-SERVE.

The clothing was sectioned and arranged in long rows of hangers and tables, wall shelving and glass cases, suits in one place, pajamas in another, shirts another, and so on, neatly arranged but ordinary.

At the moment there seemed to be no one else in the store; not even a clerk was visible. Presumably, this latter would dart forth from his vantage point when the self-serving customer had made his self-served selection.

That turned out to be not so. Chip chose a pair of pajamas, several pairs of socks, two shirts, and a dark blue suit. He carried these to the cash register, took out his billfold, rang up the total cost—accurately—deposited the money into the well-filled register, took his change, and closed the register. Humming softly to himself, he thereupon placed the suit in a cardboard carrying box, slipped the other articles into a plastic bag, and left the store, whistling now.

As Chip, outside again, presently got into a bus, the Ig hovered close to him. He was baffled to observe that Chip was one of the passengers who did not pay. Instead, he muttered two obscure monosyllables to the driver. The words sounded like, "Want spell?"

"Doubt," came the equivalent laconic answer. "Jackson Street."

"Mursev," said Chip.

Whereupon, he walked on into the bus without a backward glance, and sat down.

Did he know the driver? Was it a signal he had spoken? The Ig wondered.

If so, it was not repeated. If the two—the youth and the man—were acquainted, it didn't show. Chip finally pressed the button, and got out at the rear entrance of the bus. At Mursev street. He did not look around, or wave, after the manner of the members of this race in dealing with what they called friends. In short, he gave no additional signals of any observable kind.

The Ig had a feeling that he had witnessed a phenomenon of the system by which this society maintained its public transport. But he had failed to analyze its meaning.

There will be criticism he thought. They will say I called the fleet too soon. At the moment it looked as if the conquerors would never know certain important details of the civilization they were about to destroy.

Chip was walking rapidly along Mursev street, and presently he turned into his sister's house. He bounded up the steps, paused at the door, opening it softly. But he was evidently not silent enough; for his sister's voice reached out from the kitchen.

"Chip!"

"Yeah?" The youth paused, resignedly.

"You're home?"

"I guess you could say that."

"John wants to talk to you. He's in the living room."

"Okay," he said glumly.

With a sigh, Chip turned and walked into the living room. It was not a location that he ever sought willingly. Something about the settee, chairs and the wall TV opposite the door generally kept him standing awkwardly, or moving steadily, until he was away from the deadness of it. Perhaps the possibility of having to speak to his sister or her husband had something to do with it.

Now, as he entered, the corner of his eyes noted John at the far end of the room in the act of lowering his newspaper; but his attention lighted on an opened book lying face down on the dull coffee table. The title on one side of the backing, *The Book of Truth,* brought a twist to his mouth. Not a smile. Not a sneer. Simply a critical reaction.

He reached down and distastefully picked up the volume. As he held it, and looked down at it at closer range, his expression *was* a sneer, or perhaps a cynical contempt. He said aloud, scathingly, " 'The Book of Truth'—for God's sake. It takes an anarchistic society to feel it has finally got reality nailed down."

His brother-in-law, across the room, stared at him in surprise. "I always had the impression," he said, "that you were a dedicated adherent."

"I'm unbrainwashing myself," explained Chip. "They really clobbered me in school with this junk."

"After all," John shrugged, "if you don't like the daily version, you can always find a modified variety in one of the educational communities."

"Yeah," sneered Chip. "Even the way a place like that is named is designed to make you feel like a stupe." He mimicked in a ridiculing tone, "Educational communities."

There was a pause. Then: "You really got alienated out there in space," said the older man, slowly. "That's why I wanted to talk to you. Did you register?"

There must have been something in his voice as he asked the question; because this time Chip paused.

Finally: "You mean, there was some doubt about me on that level?"

"Not exactly." A faint smile. "But if you're that antagonistic to the *status quo*, the interviewer would probably notice, and just might refuse you right there."

Chip's expression, then, indicated to the Ig that he was remembering his verbal exchange with the interviewing girl. The memory seemed to include a thought that he had got the better of the altercation. And in fact a moment later he said with a reminiscent smile, "I think I came through all right."

"Good. That's all I wanted to know. Thanks." John leaned back, and started to raise his paper.

"What bothers me—" began Chip. He stopped and stood there, looking oddly tense, as if one part of him was struggling to finish the sentence, and another part struggling to prevent it.

The older man had evidently heard, for he now lowered his paper, looked up, and said, "Yes?"

Chip hesitated, and then began carefully, "A proper State, representing the truth of things, should be able to ensure that all citizens are protected from bodily harm, from their own impulse to harm others, and from—" Once more, he paused, and seemed to be straining.

By God, thought the Ig abruptly, he's trying to say that a State should also protect its citizens from outside invasion. . . . But of course, *all* of the returned men had, in their conditioning, been forbidden to say anything about *that*.

John clearly had no awareness of the inner torment of his youthful brother-in-law, for he now said, "That was one area where the rightists were quite properly over-ruled. They wanted much stronger punishment for people who were impelled to commit crimes. Their attitude was that a harmful act was an act of will; whereas, of course, the psychologists and sociologists had long since given up special theories on causes, and had agreed among themselves that the source of criminal impulses was unknown. Historically, murderers, thieves, and their kind were jailed or executed, because something had to be done to protect the populace. But it was a great day for basic truth when the Kirlians were interposed between someone's need to do violence and his intended victim. With that, the rightists accepted a society in which there are no jails and no gallows, but where there are educational communities. Among the varieties of such communities the alienated person can find a level of existence that matches the inner storms that torment him."

"It's really quite cut and dried" said Chip. "No loopholes, eh?" His tone was sarcastic.

John said, "It would be at its most ideal if each offender would realize the exact mental and emotional condition that troubles him, and if he would himself seek out the educational community that fits his inner needs."

"Like," said Chip, "putting all the people who won't bathe into the same educational community."

"That's where they are," was the reply. "There, the Kirlians leave them alone, women as well as men."

"Or," continued Chip, "all the people who plug up public toilets."

John grinned. "I really don't know where they're put."

"Probably in the same place as the people who repeatedly leave cigarette stubs burning in ash trays."

"Personally," said his brother-in-law, "if I were a Tech, who monitored that kind of thing, I'd put the non-bathers with the people who urinate or defecate in public places, and with individuals who get a kick out of sticking their thumbs in somebody else's coffee, milk, soft drink, or liquor."

Chip said, "I guess we've all got our special peeves. I think we could include the guy who keeps someone else from using a bathroom because he deliberately overstays."

John shrugged. "It's one of the minor harassments like cheating at cards and opening someone else's mail."

"Or kissing a girl against her will."

"That," said the older man, "begins to get close to violence. After all the Kirlians react to a threat of rape as if it's first-class intent-to-harm physically."

The youth said, "Is there any record in history of a man about to commit a crime going to jail and asking to be locked up?"

The man pursed his lips. "I believe there were a few such incidents, but so far as I know there was no legal framework wherein a person could commit himself to jail. In those days, he *could* commit himself to a mental institution."

John continued, "Actually, at least fifty percent of the residents of the educational communities did realize their problem, and did go there of their own free will."

There was a long silence. The older man finally

seemed to accept it as permanent, for he presently resumed reading.

Chip put *The Book of Truth* face down and open as he had found it, and began to back toward the hall door. At the door he paused frowning, "You have a point, sir," he said. "I could still end up at an educational community." He grinned. "That would really be the ultimate joke."

John said, "Huh?" And then he started to lower his paper again, saying, "How do you mean?"

But Chip was gone.

As he started up the stairs, his sister called, "There's a phone number on your desk. A man called about an hour ago. He said it was very important."

The youth paused, made a face, and echoed, "Important. To whom?" But he said it half to himself, and a moment later continued on up the stairs, and so to his room.

He was clearly curious, for he walked to the phone and picked up the memo that was there with the number written on it. There was no name—the Ig noticed—just the number. Chip shredded the paper with his fingers. "That for you," he said aloud, grinning, "I don't answer anonymous phone calls." He bent down carefully, and dropped the shreds into the wastepaper basket.

As he straightened, the phone rang. Cheerfully, the youth lifted the receiver, and cheerfully uttered his normal greeting: "Gluk!" And then he said, "Yep, I'm Chip Mitchum." His next words were, "Let me understand this, you're the guy that phoned and left his number." Smoothly. "I just walked into the room, and hadn't had a chance to return your call. Okay, now, who are you?"

This time there was quite a silence; and the Ig, who unhappily could not hear what was being said at the other end, waited for a clue. Finally, it came, as Chip said politely, "There must be some mistake, sir." Another pause. "If I'm guilty of such an attack, then the Kirlians should have penalized me." Pause. "I think we should end this conversation. You've got the wrong man. . . . You say the robot took a picture of me. I find that hard to believe, since I wasn't there; and so if it has a picture it would be interesting to know when it was taken, and where. You mustn't always trust a robot, you know. They have limitations." Still another pause, then firmly, "Very well, you may do anything you see fit to do, but don't bother me again with such a fanciful tale. Goodbye."

With that, he replaced the receiver, and sat on the edge of the bed with a faint frown on his goodlooking face. He was still in that position when the half-open door was pushed all the way open, and Hank stepped into the room.

Chip looked up. "We should have gone to the home of that guy I was going to beat up the other night, and got a robot likeness instead. He just phoned me."

"What's he want?" The older man sounded impatient.

"Said he was going to report me!"

"Yeah." Hank's expression was suddenly amusement. "Who to?" he asked in a ridiculing tone.

"You got me," Chip shrugged.

Hank was abruptly tolerant, even smug. "That's one thing about an anarchistic state. Nobody to report to." His grin widened. He waved a hand dismissingly. "Don't give it another thought. He can tell the whole sad story to his next door neighbor, and it won't get him anywhere."

Chip said uneasily, "I have an idea we haven't heard the last of this."

"What will he do? Come over and beat you up? If he walks along the street with such an intent, the first Kirlian he comes to will take care of him." Hank broke off. "Hal wants us to come over."

"Yeah. What for?"

"He's got some money for you."

"Huh!" Chip leaned forward, with a for-God's-sake expression on his face. He sank back, shaking his head. "I don't get it. Why does Hal want to give me money?"

"He asked you to try on a few beatings for size, and you did it. So you get some jam."

"It didn't work out too well. For my pains, I lost my ability to control the Kirlians."

The older man walked forward. "C'mon, Chip, it's Hal's way of making up the loss. Any dealings you have with Hal you can always stop right now, and never see him again. That's the beauty of an anarchistic state. No obligations to anyone."

Chip was scowling. "Where does Hal make his money?"

"Why don't you ask him when we get over there."

"Okay, okay." The youth climbed to his feet, and walked to the hall door. A moment later, as the two—Chip and Hank—arrived at the head of the stairs, Dodie came out of the kitchen, saw them and called, "Chip, a car with Mike and Dave in it just drove into the back yard. Are you all going to be here for dinner?"

Hank made a face, but Chip said cheerfully, "No, sis, we'll all be going over to Hal's." He bounced down the stairs, and down the back corridor. "See you later!" he called over his shoulder.

The older man came down more sedately. As Dodie disappeared into the kitchen, Hank called after her, "Sorry to miss your dinner, Mrs. Scheim. You're a better cook than that robot Hal has over at his place."

There was no reply, and he also then strode down the back corridor and out the rear door.

EIGHT

A HUMAN being, decided the watcher, makes a very small impingement on the world.

Lacking the Lateran Unity, or equivalent, he knows a few people only. So, always, it was the same faces around him, the same thoughts spoken over and over, and the same locations.

It was an endless repetitive stereotype.

Accordingly, here were the same four people together again, driving in the same car—Hank's—bound for a destination to which they had already gone once since their return from space.

That, thought the Slua-Ig, is what has confined me to a narrow view of this civilization—his early decision to let Chip go where he wished had had the underlying assumption that within a reasonable time the youth would take him to, or near, everything that needed to be perceived.

It was not a fateful error of judgment. Because there was still time to rectify it. But error, indeed, it had been.

The alien's first attempt at rectification was stimulated by the sight of a restaurant sign. . . . *In there*, he gently inserted his directive thought.

Getting Chip to want to go to a restaurant (so he

could observe how food was distributed in its last stage) was not a proof of total control. But it was good enough. The method reached to the conscious mind by a devious route. It pretended to be the individual's own idea. Thus, if it were within the frame of his moral code, or if he could be nudged to consider it reasonable, he would be available for many actions of a relatively neutral nature.

Within instants after Chip expressed his wish, Hank sent him a startled look. Seconds after that he had pulled over to the curb, and stopped the motor. "You've got to be kidding," he said. "For God's sake, Chip, Hal has real food. And you know what those cafes serve."

Chip shrugged. "Look, pal," he said, "I've been eating gook for four years. I've learned to like it. Besides, I want time to think about Hal."

Perfect, thought the Ig . . . Experiments on a cross section of the fleet crew had established that, after mind control was achieved, the subjects made their own rationalizations for their behavior. No suggested explanation was required.

There was a long silence from Hank. It was so long that Mike volunteered from the rear seat, "Chip, you've really given Hal's flunky a dilemma. Here's Hank, always ready to do or die for his boss, Hal. Suddenly, he's got to make his own decision, and is it tough!"

The words must have reached through whatever barriers Hank had between him and the world. His hand came up, and wiggled irritably at Mike. Another silence. Then: "Just a minute, Chip."

He opened the door on his side, climbed out and walked over to the restaurant window. He stood there, and he seemed to be reading the menu that was posted on the glass. It was getting dusk now; and so his body was slightly stooped, as if for better seeing.

Watching him from inside the car, Mike leaned toward Chip and said, "Think maybe he's getting orders through some ear receiver from Hal."

Chip grinned. "I think you do Hank wrong, Mike. He's a grown man with a lot of experience, and out there in space he worked out that whole Kirlian control thing without any help or advice from Hal."

Mike scowled. "Yeah. Like I said we're going to talk about that soon. . . ."

He said something else. But the Slua-Ig had departed, and didn't hear what it was. His perception arrived in the vicinity of Hank in time to hear the older man say, "You told me to report anything unusual. So this isn't big. But it's funny."

The answer was not audible; but it must have been non-committal; for Hank said, "Okay." Whereupon, he walked back to the car, opened Chip's door on the curb side, and said, "All right, let's eat."

" . . . No waiters," said Mike. He sounded disappointed.

They had entered the restaurant by the front door, and stood now at a little gate that separated new arrivals from the participating customers. Participation—the Ig observed—consisted of standing in a lineup with a plate, waiting for one's turn at a large machine, which held out a number of spigots. These resembled the udders of a cow; so much so that people actually had to squeeze to get the paste-like substance that came out.

Chip had his grin. "You got the wrong thought, boy," he said to Mike. "You got spoiled on that space pleasure cruise you took, with all those robot servants."

Mike shrugged, and walked through the gate. He picked up a plate, and stepped into the lineup. He watched despisingly as the people ahead of him put in coins, held up plates, and squeezed surrogate udders.

As Chip came up behind him, Mike continued, "I'd like to know what that gourmet dinner is made of."

"The menu is posted right up there in front of your eyes," Chip pointed out.

Again, Mike seemed not to hear. "What's the matter with all these shopkeepers?" he complained. "Looks as if they'd rather pay the Insect tithe than hire anybody. Where're people gonna get jobs if these S.O.B.'s hire machinery instead of humans?"

As Mike shuffled on, muttering something, Hank turned and said, "That's not Chip's problem. He can work for Hal, if he wants to. And so could you, if you'd tone down on some of those anti-anarchist ideas. Hal is for the system."

He was scowling, and the line had moved on away from him. So that Hank, standing just behind Chip, now stepped past both of them, holding his plate with one hand and fumbling in his pocket for coins with the other, moved on to the line several yards away.

"So am I," Mike retorted, "but I don't quite picture Hal as my ideological brother. I keep thinking that nobody's ever explained what happened to the guys on that first expedition Hal and Chip's brother-in-law were on ten years ago."

Hank was at the first of the udders, and said nothing more. Mike watched the gruel that came out and spread over Hank's plate like a paste, and he cringed, and was silent, remaining that way while he, also, filled his plate from the same spigots. A few minutes later, they were all sitting at a table, shoveling in forkfuls and spoonfuls of what had been posted as: crude protein (not less than 20%), crude fat (not less than 7%), crude fiber (not less than 3%), ash (not more than 7½%), and moisture (not more than 30%), plus, of course, nineteen vitamins and minerals, and the essence of thirty-two vegetables and artificial flavorings each about .01%.

"I'm not a mathematician," said Mike, as he swallowed the goo, "but I can't help noticing that no matter how you add up the posted percentages, allowing 2½% for vitamins and that other junk, it still doesn't come to more than 70%."

"You got some socialist ideal knocking around in your head," said Chip. "Capitalist anarchists are politically extreme rightists. If you don't like the food served in their cafes, start up your own. Hire waiters, serve steaks and real fish, stand behind the cash register yourself and smile at the customers. Do you know what'll happen? They'll complain that the meat was tough, and tell you to stop advertising fresh fish when, in fact, it wasn't even thawed out properly on the plate. Whereas, this tasty crude protein and crude fat. . . ." He stared down at what was left of the grayish-yellow paste, and tried to fixate a fond expression on his face, ". . . is never tough, and always comes out warm. In this society you got to take responsibility for what you believe. You're free, but there's no welfare. Everything has to be earned."

"What about the insect tax?" asked Mike.

"That's an incentive, for God's sake, to keep you responsible."

"Some people like the stuff."

"Okay, they got it. To each his own."

"Still, it's a deviation. It's welfare of sorts."

"The anarchistic substitute for unemployment insurance," said Chip, with a dismissing wave of one hand and arm. "Not the same at all."

It grew darker outside the window beside which they sat. The Ig, hovering just above Chip, noticed that Mike's grumblings didn't seem to be meaningful even to him; for he dutifully cleaned up his plate, including using a spoon to scoop up final soupy remnants.

The alien thought: the members of this race are so disorganized mentally that even Hank seems to have forgotten that Chip explained the stopover so that he could "think" about Hal . . . and that subject had never come up again.

Naturally, Ig precision logic still required that the deadly game was not complete until the way of life of these people was understood. By the rules of Ig gameplaying, as modified for these confusing human beings, that meant that he really ought to find out facts to make a good showing. For himself.

There seemed to be nothing more to learn here.

And yet as the foursome emerged from the restaurant, a red light was flashing on the meter of Hank's car.

Mike grinned at Chip. "You can see how far gone Hank was when we arrived," he said. "Forgot to put money in for parking. Now, he has to go through the ritual."

The three youths stood by amused while Hank did the ritual." Like everybody else had learned to do, Hank re-read the instructions. They were complicated, and people had a tendency to forget the precise order of the seven steps that, when achieved exactly, would enable the car's motor to start again.

Mike continued to make slighting comments; and so at least a portion of the sad story of human dereliction that had made the complex parking meters necessary, came through to the watching alien.

The parking meter system was privately owned. They had been installed by an agreement between the Caps, the Co-ops, and the Techs. A percentage of drivers had turned out to be totally without consideration. Employees of nearby businesses would park all day on the street in congested areas. In the early years of anarchism, people often left their cars in the middle of a main thoroughfare for hours or days, and the traffic edged around them, sometimes backed up for a dozen blocks.

The release ritual, as the Ig observed it closely, was: First, unlock the driver's door and open it. Second, put transmission in low gear. Third, place correct fee in parking meter—based on 1 cent a minute. Fourth, put gear in Park position. Fifth, insert penalty of 25¢ in parking meter. Sixth, get into car and place full weight of body on driver's seat. Seventh, wait for release buzz to sound from parking meter.

(Motor will now start.)

NINE

THE ARRIVAL AT Hal's was sudden. They drove up.
They turned into and along a tree-lined driveway and
ended in a large courtyard—brightly lighted, almost
garish, but rich looking.

The Ig had intended to survey the approaches to
the house with the care of a dedicated gameplayer.
But there they abruptly were at journey's end; and he
had failed to deduce from anyone's reaction that this
particular fine house in this street of fine residences
was the place.

The alien could only conclude that the three
youths, having been to Hal's but one time, had had no
warning either. Hank, of course, had known Hal and
the way here for over a decade; and so he was the
finder, and the arriver who took his advance knowledge for granted. And, hence, gave no signals.

Oh, well, all I really want is a close view of Hal,
and a chance to probe into his enigmatic mind.

The scramble to get out of the car and follow a
hightailing Hank into Hal's house was equally swift
and perceptively non-productive for the Ig observer.
Inside, the view was immediately familiar to
everyone, including the alien. Hank simply pushed
open the rear door, and there was a short anteroom,

and then the large elegantly furnished drawing room.

Hank raised his voice with loud familiarity, "Hey, Hal, where are you?"

There was no immediate direct reply. But the Ig whose perception had floated into that luxurious room slightly ahead of Chip, saw there were occupants. Hank and he seemed to become aware of them simultaneously. Hank slowed and muttered something under his breath. The Ig, being so close to the man, heard the mumbled words. They were: "For God's sake, those nobodies still here!"

The four occupants of that glittering room were youths of the same age level as Chip and Mike and Dave. But there the resemblance ended. The four did not turn, or indicate by any movement that they were conscious of the new arrivals. They sat in a tight group at the far end of the room. They had jockied priceless chairs and settees so close together that even their knees touched. Yet the aspect they presented was not so much of a physical proximity as of some kind of intimacy of the soul.

Chip, a grin on his face, stepped past Hank and approached the foursome who for the entire minute or so that had passed, had been audibly engaged in a verbal interchange that totally absorbed them. After he had listened for half a minute, Chip turned his head and called out:

"We should've dragged along Walt and Don. They got soulmates here."

Mike and Dave walked over, and the Ig floated with them. As his perception came within hearing distance, he heard one of the four say, "The mental picture I have is of lying on my back on the floor—"

"Same, me," shuddered Two. "It's like a bad

dream. Lyin' there with one of those four-leggers bending over me with a syringe—''

Chip was walking on, but the Ig held himself back, and listened with a rising alarm.

''And there was a machine saying something loud right into my ear,'' breathed Three. ''I don't remember if it spoke English—''

''From where I lay, I could see my whole outfit, everybody flat on his back, with those slinky things wheeling machinery from one to the other to t'other . . .'' moaned Four.

On far Slua, the astounded Ig trembled. What he had listened to was a breakthrough from the lower levels of the mind, of truth. But how? And everyone of the four equally aware at the same instant of time. It should have been impossible.

Mike was shaking his head, and he quickly walked on. Only Dave, of the three arriving youths, stayed behind, frowning, and looking baffled. Abruptly, he also moved away. The Ig perception followed him as he hastened after Mike.

A moment later Dave said in a low voice to Mike, ''Those guys are nuts. Somebody must be brainwashing them into thinking that things happened that didn't happen at all.''

''Sssshh,'' said Mike, ''there's Hal.''

A door off to the left in the far corner had opened. Out of it charged a bearded, chunky man about five feet nine in height. ''Hey!'' he said in a deep baritone.

He strode over to Chip, who was closest, and grabbed his hand, waggled it in what was obviously intended to be a shake. Even as he did so, he stepped past Chip and up to Hank, and grabbed his hand, also.

Belatedly, then, he waved at Dave and Mike. "Hi, fellows!"

Yes, indeed, there was Hal. But the Ig noted that, although Dave waved back, Mike merely moved his lips; no words of return greeting actually issued forth. Instead, he stared at their host sourly, and finally muttered in an aside to Dave, "Yeah, and we can guess that there's the brainwasher."

Mike added, "I'm hoping we can steer Chip away from this place and these two before very long."

"I see what you mean," said the red-headed ex-farm boy.

Like Chip and Mike and Dave, the Ig had, so to say, met Hal Steggars once before. That first night after the fleet returned, only five short days ago, Hank had brought Chip and his chums (and of course the accompanying Ig perception) to a party in this bright, gleaming house.

There were other returnees present, including the obsessed foursome—and several duos and trios like them who huddled into their separate corners. And, like a breath of fresh air to the relatively normal types among the male guests, there was present an abundance of girls.

Presumably, the girls were there of their own free will, and were not purchased items. Though it was a little odd that not one of them said no, or even hesitated, when requested by an eager youth to disappear with him into one of a row of bedrooms.

Of all the . . . normal . . . returnees, only Mike refused to disappear into a bedroom. He was actually approached by a black girl, but he shook his head. Naturally, the obsessed historians of the expedition—the foursome in one corner, and their soul brothers in other huddles—did not even appear to be aware that there were girls in the room.

On this second visit, no girls were in sight.

But there was Hal smiling behind or through his beard. His was one of the bush style beards. The entire lower part of his face was a brownish clump of protruding hair. Concealed in that small forest, the mouth was fleetingly visible only when he opened it.

Which he now did—open it, that is. The mouth said, "Come on into the bar, fellows."

Moments later, there they were, surrounded by red plush walls and gleaming mirrors; and Hal behind the bar peering out at them from somewhere to the rear of his beard. He was professional and courteous, eliciting from each in turn what drink he would like, and thereupon doing a quick mix and serve.

Hal raised his own glass, clinked it to Chip's and then to Hank's, and waved it vaguely toward Mike and Dave, and said, "Here's to brave men and stout hearts!"

Only Mike hesitated as the toast was offered. He stood as the others drank, then shrugged, and said, "Can't really argue with that, can you?" Whereupon he lifted his glass and sipped from it.

Hal was putting his glass down. He stood there, a chunky type, with blue eyes that were unusually alert, and slightly narrowed now, as if the brain behind was making one more assessment, one final reconsideration of a previously arrived at plan. Abruptly, whatever was going on inside the head, completed. The eyes opened wide. The beard separated, and the voice from inside it said, "Chip, these last few days, since you landed, you must've thought about what it's like to live on the edge of the Kirlians."

It was instantly observable (by the alien) that the youth was uncertain about how to reply to the statement. He stroked his jaw. He stared at Hal. Then: "I don't know what you're getting at."

"For a few days after you got back, you had protection—right?"

Chip nodded warily.

"None of them," urged Hal, "could touch you?"

Once again, Chip nodded.

"Felt pretty good, didn't it?"

"Well, in a way. But I also felt guilty. It seemed . . ." he hesitated, "as if nobody ought to have that advantage."

"You damned right they shouldn't!" came the voice of Mike.

Somewhere within the beard a faint smile seemed to be forming. "Mike," said Hal, in an amazingly goodnatured tone, "what you don't understand is that every rigidity should have a proven crack in it. Then, if something goes wrong, determined men can go in and break it up. Chip proved we can do it one way, and I've pretty well proved we can do it another. That makes me feel better."

"How you prove it?" asked Mike, pointedly. "We know how Chip did. What other way is there?"

Chip said, "What's this edge you talkin' about?"

"You went over it," the beard murmured. "What happened?"

"I got zapped."

"Right." Triumphantly. "And you can only do

that once, because the second penalty hits hard."

"Whatcha gettin' at?" said Chip.

"You gotta learn all your lessons the first zap," came the grinning response. "So I learned that lesson when I was on the first expedition ten years ago. As a starter I became a deep trance subject."

"You mean—hypnotism?"

The beard waggled. The face behind it twisted into what looked like a dismissing smile. Hal said, "What goes on in a human being when, suddenly, he has to do what the hypnotist says, is a little more complex than used to be thought."

"So, all right," Chip persisted, "like everything else it's got a deep thing behind it. But—"

"No buts," said Hal curtly. "I thought it all through before I made my first test on that first expedition—you know what I did?" It was a rhetorical question, it turned out; for he answered it immediately. He said, "I trained myself so I am not subject to the Kirlians."

Mike put his drink down on the bar's leather top. "You're kidding!" he said incredulously.

"When I get mad enough to do violence," said Hal smugly, "the Kirlians think I'm laughing."

"That's big talk," said Mike sharply. "Suppose'n you try to kill somebody—what then?"

Hal drew a deep breath. The beard held quite steady as he did so. "Mike," he said slowly, "sometimes men still have to be killed. I killed eleven men to get where I am today. It could be that the guy that tipped off the Kirlian control group the other night against Chip will be Number Twelve."

There was silence. Mike picked up his glass; and his hand was trembling as he took a drink. Finally:

"You're sure talkin' rough, man. What's the emergency?"

The blue eyes were narrowed to slits. "Mike, there's something awful strange about the way the second expedition handled itself out there in space. And something even stranger about the story it brought back."

"All right, so you call a public meeting, and tell 'em your suspicions."

"That's for the slow moving herd. Just like the talk on the media. I'm not waiting for the response on that, Mike. And I'm not showing my head in public for somebody to knock off."

"Okay, what you do? Why you tellin' us this? What's brewin' here?" Mike had been drinking rapidly. Now, he set his glass on the bar. "I need another one of those. I'm feelin' nervous all over. You gonna offer us to be your front men?"

Hal took the glass in a deliberate way, poured and mixed, and shoved back, and then said coolly, "Not you, Mike. Chip."

"And Hank?" asked Mike.

"Hank," said the determined voice, "I've already got enrolled."

"Yeah, I guessed that," said the black youth.

Hal seemed not to hear. His gaze had shifted to Chip's face. Abruptly, he came around the bar, took hold of that individual's arm, and said softly, "Chip, you come with me. I'd like you to meet an expert. And I'd like us to have a confab."

"Watch it, pal," warned Mike.

"No harm in a little confab," said Chip, casually. "And I'm curious to know what kind of expert this guy thinks is an expert."

As Chip walked briskly with Hal to the door behind the bar, Mike called out urgently, "We've been gettin' some straight talk here tonight, fella. Never heard anything like it in my life. Be careful what you agree to."

The alien was floating after Chip—who was already partly through the door—when there was a sound. It was the sound of a door opening suddenly. The door by which Hal and Hank and the three youths had, a short time before, entered the bar.

Through that open door a long line of men ran into the room.

The man in the lead yelled at Chip and Hal: "Hey, you two, stop!"

Chip had paused, and glanced back, startled. The muscular Hal didn't even look. His already firm hold of Chip's arm tightened. Now, Chip in hand, so to speak, he lunged. The next instant the two of them were through that rear door. With a synchronized follow-through movement with his other hand, Hal pulled the door shut after him. It closed with a metallic click.

And it really closed. Because the intruders were at it within seconds. The first man to hit it with his body pulled back in pain. "It's steel," he moaned. Whatever it was, it was unbudgeable.

The Ig lingered long enough to become aware that the leader of the invading group looked familiar. After moments only, recognition came. It was the individual Chip had intended to assault several evenings ago—and had, instead, been confronted by a robot duplicate. The same man who had phoned Chip this very afternoon, and threatened him with exposure.

As the alien, hastily now—for he had a sense of Chip receding—floated through the door, there seemed to be no question . . . I'm at the right place—Whatever opposition might develop on earth against the imminent Ig invasion, one of the starting points was right here.

TEN

THE IG found himself in a wide hallway facing an elevator shaft. No one was in sight; that was the immediate first impression.

There could be no time to examine these new surroundings. The downward tug feeling apprised the alien that Hal and Chip were on their way to a deep basement. Or at least Chip was moving farther in that direction each instant. The Slua-Ig deduced that the two human beings had simply stepped straight into an open elevator, and headed down.

He moved after them, sinking through a steel floor into an upper basement, and then through another steel floor to a sub-basement. And there, indeed, was Chip, and with him, the heavy-set man. They were in the act of stepping out of the elevator into another hallway.

It was suddenly amazing, then, that neither individual seemed concerned about what was taking place two floors above them. For all they knew, the intruders were confronting Hank, Mike, and David. And what was amazing was that Chip had, until now, seemed to be the type of person who was concerned about the welfare of his friends.

He showed no sign of concern. He was sauntering toward a closed door directly behind Hal. The man, being first to arrive, touched a space in the wall beside the door. It glided open weightily. More metal, evidently. The older man stepped aside and motioned to Chip, who, thereupon, walked into the room. The Ig was now slightly in the lead. He was aware of Hal bringing up the rear; and conscious also that the man paused to touch the inside wall and remained there until the heavy door had glided shut, and clicked into its lock.

Impressions from in front, next.

First, the shape and three dimensional presence of another man. He was standing beside a long table. Everywhere was the effect of over-bright lights in a large room filled with machinery and instruments.

Too much. Too many focus points.

It was an all too common limitation on utilizing the perception of another being at a vast distance. The Ig accepted the curtailment. And, so to speak, poised near Chip. And waited.

Hal's house was definitely a place to take note of. The sophistication of equipment hidden in this lower section implied that this man was ready for action. Implied some knowledge of the truth; or at least suspicion of it.

Not that it mattered, of course, except as a stimulant to the game. Only nine days plus a few hours remained to mankind.

The man standing by the long table in the foreground inclined his head in greeting.

He was well dressed, by human standards. He looked fortyish, capable. He said to Chip, "Look around you. We're in a safe place."

Chip had walked forward indolently, and stopped. Now, he stared directly at the man's face, and did not glance sideways or up or down. "I've looked," he said. Pause. Silence. Then, he added, "Safe in what way?"

"From being spied on," said the man, simply.

"By whom?"

The gray gaze of the man and the blue of the youth interlocked for a long moment. It was Chip who presently glanced away.

The man said, "Chip, something is wrong, and you're connected to it. But down here—" He waved vaguely with one hand, presumably indicating the equipment around them—"is everything we need to prevent what we're going to talk about being overheard."

Toward the finish of his little speech he had lowered his voice. And the Ig, anxious not to miss a word, moved along Chip's perception until he was between the two human beings.

Chip did not reply immediately. Instead, he walked around the table and over to a bank of instruments that spread across one wall and all the way from the ceiling to the floor. The slightly cynical smile that had been his expression all these minutes, faded from his face. He said in astonishment: "One of those universal mind expansion systems! *Here*!"

"Where else but Hal's?" said the man.

"But where do you get the power to run it?"

"Where does Hal get anything?" Once more the answer was in the form of a question.

"We had one of these on each ship," said the youth. I played around with our unit a little, but stayed below eight percent expansion."

"Early memories in your own life?"

Chip nodded. "A few prenatal, but mostly only as far back as infancy. People looked huge."

"The giants in ancient fairy stories," acknowledged the man, "were probably the adults of a baby's world." He added, "Why didn't you go deeper?"

Chip shrugged. "I'm one of these people who like to stay in control. Of my actions. Of my body. Of my memories. In short," he grinned, "a genuine rightist anarchist. But I did work the machine on guys who didn't have my restrictions. So I heard the usual strange stories."

"Oh!" Surprise. "Then you know how to operate this?"

Chip did not reply with words. Instead, he reached over to a bank of dials, touched one, pressed another, turned a third." His body stiffened. He let go, and stood there, shuddering.

Behind him, the man said softly, "I was going to ask if I could connect you. But you've done it yourself."

There was no immediate reply. At least another minute went by, at which time Chip seemed to have control of the shiver effect. He said finally, "I have the feeling that I'll need all the support I can get during the next few weeks. Maybe continuous therapy on a low level is what the doctor would have ordered if there was one."

"Be sure to take plenty of B-complex and protein," said the older man. "Nothing like the right food for proper repair of the body cells during therapy."

Chip said, "I'm hoping in the crunch this thing can keep me alive."

"If you stay in the city, the way you've got it set will do it right now. But the farther away you go, the more power it takes."

Chip sighed. "Yeah, I know."

"But for that you will need a preliminary adjustment period where you'd just sleep. Call Hal when you have the time for that."

Chip said, "That's the big problem. Time. But—" he nodded—"I'll call Hal." He glanced over to where the chunky man waited silently. "Time we got you back into this conversation, Hal."

"It's okay," said Hal, "I'll stand by till I'm needed."

Chip turned his back on the instrument board, with its complex of transistorized circuits, and walked toward the table, from the opposite side now. Reaching it, he drew out one of the chairs, and sat down directly across from where the stranger was standing. He jerked his arm, pointing upward with his thumb. "You listen to what those four bats upstairs are saying?"

The man said, "I'm the guy that released the buried memories."

Having spoken, he pulled out the chair nearest to him, and sank into it, facing Chip. "They tell an interesting story, don't they?" he said.

"It looks like we were all captured," said Chip, "and indoctrinated."

"You were indeed."

"Including me," said Chip.

The man nodded, non-committally, but made no verbal answer. As they sat there silent staring at each other, Hal, who had been waiting unobtrusively in the background, came forward, pulled out an end chair, and settled weightily into it. "Don't mind me," he said.

If the dialogists heard him, it didn't show. Chip continued, "With me it didn't take. I remembered it all, minute by minute."

The man said, "It's amazing how when you have a large enough group the statistical reality is that some are affected one way, some another, and some appear to be immune."

"I watched some of the immunes being killed," said Chip. "The indoctrination didn't take on them, and they weren't smart enough to conceal it."

"There may be a few others like you," said the man.

Pause. Then: "Who are you?" said Chip. "And why are we having this conversation?"

"I'm a psychiatrist," was the reply. "I don't think it would be wise to give you my name."

"We were defeated," said Chip, "by an enemy who apparently understood in a very superior way what goes on in a human being."

"They understood something," said the psychiatrist, "and understood it well. But in a way we understand it better."

There must have been a negating thought in Chip's expression; for he went on quickly, "All right, all right, I agree. If we're so smart how come they were able to overwhelm an entire fleet, and in a simple way control everybody's mind?"

The doctor shrugged. "The fact is, our society being what it is, nobody had taken responsibility for that bit of knowledge. No doctor or psychologist said in advance, 'Let's assume these aliens have superior understanding of the human nervous system. How are we going to defend ourselves from their knowledge?' "

Chip relaxed, frowned, nodded. "Okay," he said, "I get it. The price of every man doing as he pleases sometimes leaves gaps. Because of such a gap, they could have exterminated us, but instead they allowed everybody to come home in a brainwashed state. I couldn't seem to break out of part of the brainwashing—I've been unable to say anything about the alien threat. How come I can suddenly talk about it to you?"

"That's the new thought—theory—about hypnosis that I just mentioned."

"How does it work?" Frowning.

"It's what you believe of a suggestion that is hypnotically effective. In bringing you down among all this machinery, and telling you it protects you, evidently that part of your brain was convinced. So, down here in Hal's sub-sub-basement, you're free."

"You mean, maybe I'm not protected. I just think I am."

"My guess is you actually are protected," said the man but without real conviction in his tone.

"Guessing doesn't sound as certain as what you said earlier," said Chip.

"You'll have to work it out inside yourself," was the reply.

The youth's brows were knit. "Hey, I'm remembering something. Right after I had my Kirlian control taken away from me, I was in quite an emotional state; and right there I could hint at the danger, without naming it."

"That gives you some idea of the internal forces at work."

Chip seemed not to hear. "The way I worked it out earlier," he said, "when Hal suggested I beat up on a few guys, at first I thought he was out of his mind—I'd never beaten up on anybody in my life. Then I thought, hey, maybe this is a way to get attention. Maybe people will begin to wonder if somebody beats up enough guys."

"That beating-up idea was mine," said the psychiatrist. "Hal passed it along to you."

He added, "It was also my idea that you beat up Kirlian Tech A's."

Chip said, "There, you made a mistake. They showed up as stupes, wrapped up in their own power group thinking, not a thought outside their particular angle on being responsible for the Kirlians. So," he shrugged, "that was all a waste. We're not one millimeter further ahead than when we started. So, what do we do now? Basically, that means what's the real purpose of these aliens?"

The older man had listened silently to the explanation. He looked troubled. If he had any tendency to dismiss the extent of the threat, or be lulled by the facts as they had been stated, it didn't show.

He said finally, unhappily, "I'm puzzled at the extent of the control you're under. As I said, in effect, hypnotism has too shallow a meaning for the complex phenomena that has been observed from the earliest days of mind control. Consider that Mesmer believed that the effect came from magnets; and his subjects responded as if that was what was happening."

He went on, "We have to also take into account the reality of the whole problem of an individual having to learn to control his thinking with so much unnoticed influence from sub-awareness associations.

"Hypnosis operating through and with the help of such an immense clutter of mental images is . . ."

Here we go again, the far-distant Slua-Ig, in effect, groaned. . . . Earlier, a similar remark by Hal, and now the same idea from this far more authoritative source. The obvious consequence: Chip knowing and thinking about a new, deeper approach to hypnosis, might have a thought of his own about himself. Gently, the alien inserted the interfering idea. And, so to speak, sat back, triumphant.

There was abruptly boredom on Chip's face. The psychiatrist, watching him closely, said hastily, "Naturally, it will be unnecessary to go into such technical details now—"

He had lost his hearer's attention. The youth was glancing toward Hal. "You keeping track what's going on upstairs?" he asked.

Hal tapped his right ear significantly with his right index finger. "Got a little listener right in here." He shrugged. "It's you they're after. So there's no problem."

That was a perfect diversionary tactic thought the Ig. Again, Chip had found his own rationalization for letting his attention wander. A belated concern for his friends.

Chip was frowning. "What can those guys upstairs do to me if they catch me?" he asked.

"Nothing. You've paid your penalty. So the second stage reprisal doesn't apply to you until you do another violent act."

"Chip!" interjected the psychiatrist at that point. His tone was patient, but his voice was up in pitch.

"So what," asked Chip, of Hal, "did they charge over here for?"

"*Chip!*" said the psychiatrist in a more compelling tone.

"They say they want to talk to you. But truth is these Techs haven't been too bright, so I'd rather you didn't."

The youth waggled one finger in the direction of the psychiatrist, but did not look at the man. "He's tryin' to talk to me. All right, so you all talk to me, so you get me interested. Then what?"

Hal had lowered his hand to the table. His heavy face broke into a faint, cynical smile, which he directed toward the man who sat across from Chip. "Yeah, Doc," he said good naturedly, "what can he do for you? I know what he can do for me. But that's another river going to a different ocean."

"I was hoping," said the psychiatrist, "that Chip might become interested in finding out what was actually done to him."

"You mean," Chip asked puzzled, "maybe next time they'll get me?"

"No . . ." he said. "Maybe *last* time they got you. Maybe they need one or two or a dozen that think they got away."

This one approaches the truth, thought the Ig.

The first response in Chip was a surge of high color into his face. Then he stood up, and glanced at Hal. "You say you got something for me to do?"

"Yeah!" Hal spoke softly, crouching a little where he sat, watching the youth with upward slanting eyes.

"What?"

"Today is Wednesday—right?"

"Yeah."

"You probably won't hear from that college thing for a couple of days—right?"

"Right."

"Then it'll be the weekend. So nothing can happen until Monday, no matter how you slice it—sound reasonable?"

"Makes sense."

"Four days?"

"Yeah."

"During those 96 hours," said Hal, "I want you to fly over the world and look at fleet launch pads."

"And do what?"

"There're about a hundred of 'em."

"So?"

"Evaluate how many launch shuttles are on their pads, and how many are missing."

I can use that information, myself, thought the Ig.

Chip was speaking. "Sounds like a grind, but not impossible."

"Hank will go with you."

"Why not just Hank, alone?" Chip said. He was suddenly scowling. "He can count as good as me."

Hal stood up, and came around the table. He bent over the youth. "Listen, kid," he said, "it could be you'll run into something, and you call me long distance. And then we decide some action is necessary. Hank is only good for up to a certain level of action. You're good for above that level."

"What could we run into?"

The man shook his head, earnestly. "I don't know—honest. But fact is, I'm with Doc here. I'm afraid. I don't think we ought to waste any time.

There's got to be some reason why the aliens let all you guys go, after giving you the biggest brainwash that ever was."

"Yeah. That bothers me. How did they do that? How did they get aboard even one ship?"

"That information I got," interjected the psychiatrist. "Anarchism."

"Huh?" Chip knit his brows.

"A landing was made, right?"

Chip nodded. "From my ship, as a matter of fact."

"What happened?"

"Nothing. We landed near one of the poles. All snow and ice."

"So some of the guys wandered off in typical Anarchistic Style, doing as they pleased."

"As it says in the books, that's the price you have to pay for freedom."

"They were captured, indoctrinated, and then sent back. When they got aboard, they did what they had to, and so a bunch of aliens got onto the ship, and indoctrinated everybody, and then they wrecked your ship with an explosion. The blow-up killed the people they were doubtful about, and made it necessary for the survivors to be taken aboard the other ships."

"Where'd you learn all this?"

"From those guys upstairs, and others like them."

"Don't you have some line of communication to other psychiatrists to tell them what you found out?"

"I wrote up the information," said the older man, "and Hal sent it out to 83,000 psychiatrists. As a result there'll be a meeting in 9 days, where I'll present a paper, and there'll be a discussion."

Chip snarled, "Why didn't you tell those S.O.B.'s

to get up there and man the fifteen ships that's left of the fleet?"

"You don't tell another psychiatrist anything," said this psychiatrist.

"Yeah," Chip returned cynically, "just another typical group of citizens of earth, anarchistically responsible only for themselves."

"Our most exportable item," said Hal, who had walked to one side. "And you have to admit it paid off a decade ago when the Alpha Centaurus anarchists decided to pay us a visit just as the alien fleet started to drop hydrogen bombs. We told the Centaurans what was happening, and they engaged the aliens, and drove them off."

"But here we are again," said Chip, "and this time no Alpha Centaurans to the rescue. So it looks as if here on earth the anarchistic system is so unmilitary that it can't defend itself."

"Since I've still got you here," Chip went on, "another question." The words were addressed to the psychiatrist.

The bright, intelligent eyes stared at him. "Ask!"

"What's the matter with people?

"You mean, generally?"

"I mean, presumably the perfect world is here. Everybody free to do as he pleases, except he mustn't harm others. And everybody is still crazy, to some extent. After a hundred years, how come?"

The man shrugged. "That's a big question. But one answer I can give: The village idiot has been put back in the village. He's no longer in an institution. If he's harmless, he stays there. If he's violent, he finds himself with the rest of the type going down the line of educational communities. Is that what you mean?"

"No, I don't mean the outright crazy or the basket cases. I mean, literally, where does all the rage come from in ordinary people?"

"There are about eight principal schools of thought," was the smiling reply. "I subscribe to one of them. Do you want to hear it?"

"You make it sound like one-eighth of nothing," said Chip. "So, no, I guess not."

"Still," said the other, "you may be interested in learning that your observation is not new. Freud, the founder of psychoanalysis, to quote one of his biographers, 'did not have a very high opinion of the bulk of mankind. He felt that the irrational forces in man's nature are so strong that the rational forces have little chance against them.' "

Chip interjected, "I thought psychoanalysis ended up on a junkpile of unusable ideas before the end of the 20th century."

Said the psychiatrist, "Freud's technique of psychotherapy was too slow and too expensive. But his basic observations were never seriously questioned. Ferenzci, an early Freudian, summed it up when he said, 'With increasing experience one becomes convinced that the apparently motiveless extravagance of affect, the excessive hate, love, and sympathy of the neurotics, are long forgotten psychical experiences brought into connection with the current occasion. And that, also, those non-analyzed "healthy persons" who, as we know with certainty, carry about with them throughout life a multitude of repressed ideational complexes that are at all times ready to increase and exaggerate with their affect-value the pathogenic action of psychical traumata.'''

Chip said resignedly, "So alright. So everybody's got shock in him. It keeps trying to come out. And the Kirlians keep pushing it back. Pretty grim, if you ask me."

"It has been estimated," said the older man, "that even with modern techniques it would take two years per person to erase all that deeply buried hypnotism."

"I see your point." Chip spoke reluctantly. "So that means we're right back with the Kirlians playing the role of papa and mama saying, 'Naughty, naughty, spank, spank.' Pretty degrading."

The reply: "Those systems for training people to think differently work best on those who got a small dose of childhood shock, and don't work on those who accidentally got the bigger packages."

"I understand that, I think," said Chip. "However, in the present crisis we need something more than mere resistance or other automatic behavior. Therefore, Chip, it looks as if you've served your purpose in my part of this scheme."

The words were spoken in an even tone. As a consequence they, so to say, went some distance past Chip before he did a doubletake and mentally hauled them back within rehearing distance. "Just a minute," he said, "that sounds like I'm being dealt out of the proceedings."

"Out of my part," nodded the man.

There was a pause; then: "Who are you?" asked Chip.

"I've told you. I'm a psychiatrist."

"I mean, what's your role in this?"

A bleak smile crinkled the bland face. "You're the first person who's ever asked me that." The lips pursed. "Hmmm, what's my role!" The smile broadened. "Alright, I've got it. I'm the man who, if I couldn't get you and Hal to solve the problem of these aliens, will have to solve it myself."

Chip was not about to be put off by specious statements. "What do we understand better than the enemy?"

"Oh, the Kirlians, for one thing."

"They captured our ships. They must have noticed the Kirlians, and taken them apart."

"Oh!" Quietly. "All hundred or so races with an advanced technology that we've run into, have done something with the Kirlian phenomena, but no one before us realized their possibilities as total—but total—police and security substitutes."

"I still can't imagine why you had Hank connect me to the ship Kirlians, so that Kirlians everywhere allowed me special privileges."

"If," was the reply, "my life depended on answering that, I'd say you haven't proved yourself a good enough survivor for my purposes. But—" he shrugged—"you were the one Hank selected."

"Are you telling me," challenged Chip, "that a good survivor wouldn't have allowed himself to be trapped, and disconnected from those Kirlians?"

"That, also. But it goes deeper than that."

"I get it. Napoleon was a general at twenty-three. I'm only a lieutenant-colonel at twenty, with no chance for advancement."

"A real winner," nodded the psychiatrist, earnestly, "takes charge, does what he has to do, and saves the world without being told how.''

"Okay," said Chip in a resigned tone, "that's not me. I'm waiting for additional instructions."

"From whom?"

"When I took that small amount of therapy from the mind-expansion machine aboard my ship—" His thumb motioned to the machine off to one side—"I discovered that I was waiting for my dead father to start training me for life."

"How did your father die?"

"He and my mother were killed in an accident when I was eleven. Our apartment building collapsed. The architect had neglected to put in proper supports. My sister and I were in school when it happened, and were subsequently brought up by my mother's parents, who didn't appreciate the responsibility. It was my mother's father who volunteered me for the space expedition at age sixteen. I was pretty critical of him for it, and I'm not planning to visit him."

"Under all these circumstances," said the man, "in your opinion is there anything further you can do?"

"I'll have to think about it," said Chip. He was abruptly more cheerful. "I guess reality has its place, and plain talk can be useful."

"If you think of anything," was the reply, "tell Hal. He'll pass it on to me."

Hal, who had been standing by patiently, moved forward, and reminded, "Chip, you're still useful to me. We all need that information I want you to get."

The youth said, cheerfully, "Here I thought I was working for myself, and suddenly I'm fired from a job

I didn't even know I had, by a psychiatrist I didn't know existed until this evening. And suddenly I discover that I'm an employee of a man I kind've respect."

"Go home!" urged the chunky Hal. "Get a good night's sleep. Hank will come over in the morning with the airline tickets."

"How do I get home?" Chip gestured. "I mean, past that mob upstairs."

Hal indicated the psychiatrist with his thumb. "He'll drive you home."

"Does he work for you?"

"Well—no."

"Then how come you're telling him what he has to do."

Somewhere behind his beard Hal made a face. "Look," he said patiently, "there's a tunnel from here over to another house across the street. Doc has his car parked over there. Since you've brought up the subject of free will, when you walk over there with him, you can ask him for a ride. And Doc?"

"Yes?" The psychiatrist's lean face reflected an inner hesitation, as if something had just happened that he was not happy with.

"Don't put any more pressure on this guy. Okay?"

The upturned face was both disturbed and puzzled, now. Watching it, the Slua-Ig had the insight that he was witnessing here one of the basic problems of the human society. One man—Hal—was telling another man—the physician—not to do something. And in a free society—*really* free—one man didn't do that to another man.

The psychiatrist parted his lips as if to say something, but before he could speak, Hal went on in an urging voice, "You've stated your point. Let him cudgel it. Okay?"

The hesitation lasted bare moments longer. Then—decision. And acceptance. The man said quietly, "The question in my mind is, if we can't get someone like Chip, here, to take an instant interest in exploring what may have happened to him, how are we going to appeal for help to all those people out there?" He gestured with his right hand, a sweeping movement that took in half the horizon. Presumably, the gesture indicated where the people "out there" were.

He didn't seem to realize that the momentary threatening conflict between himself and Hal was, in fact, the answer to what he wanted to know. Here were two men apparently shared a common concern. And yet for a few seconds they had visibly been at odds.

All by itself that was encouraging. But for a race as determined as the Ig, it was not enough to know that man's political system had flaws in it. The question in the alien's mind was grim, and immediate. How could Chip—or one of the others like him—be used to exterminate both these men?

Quickly.

ELEVEN

CHIP AND THE psychiatrist went through a door. And the Slua-Ig deduced that the long, lighted hallway that stretched beyond that door was, in fact, the tunnel referred to by Hal. The two came presently to a stairway and that led up and through another door out to a night-darkened yard, made darker by over-hanging trees.

There was a car visible at the far rear of the yard. Not too surprisingly, the older man led the way to it, and he and Chip climbed in.

The Ig had been just a little slow; and so he had a few anxious moments. He had taken note on several occasions of a number on the front of Hank's car, and had assumed it identified the machine's ownership.

If I ever hope to locate this human being again—the psychiatrist—then a means of identification is mandatory. And so, even as the two humans got into the car, the alien perception floated to the front of the automobile. The motor coughed, and caught. The machine began to move. At which precise moment he was in front of the number. The headlights came on; and in the resultant reflections the figures stood out clearly: AG-872-31.

At the moment, of course, it was not possible to determine where or how such data was recorded in an anarchistic society. But there must be a method by which people and their property were locatable.

Somehow, find this man tomorrow. At the latest.

The automobile was turning into an alleyway, and was moving rapidly. The Ig perception lifted itself up over the hood, and through the glass. It passed between the two people in the front seat, and took up position just behind them. Poised there, ready to hear what was said if they spoke.

But the drive to the home of Chip's sister was uneventful and silent. The psychiatrist stopped the machine at the front entrance of the house, and Chip got out. He waved a cheerful goodbye, said thank you, and walked to the gate. No trees here. The moon was visible in a cloudless night sky. There were sounds; the car driving off, the youth's footsteps on the pavement and then on the veranda. The click and the rattle of the door knob. The first glimpse of the now familiar interior.

The day was, of course, about over. Theoretically, thought the alien, I could sign off right now, and trust that nothing more of interest will occur. Naturally, he wouldn't. The great game-playing lifestyle of the Ig took nothing for granted. He was never caught napping. He accepted that the enemy was really scheming all the time, waiting to catch the opponent off guard; fighting in his own slipshod fashion for survival.

We must never forget that, thought the Ig . . . Stupid though these human beings were, underneath all their stereotyped behavior was the same, bright, intense, self-admiring unit of awareness that had been observed so often in other inferior races. That intense thing waited at some core of the individual.

Waited for the clumsy neural and other organic equipment with which it perceived and manipulated the world, to evolve. Here, however, there was an anomaly. The human organic equipment was actually quite adequate. But these disorganized beings had not yet learned to utilize it optimally. . . . If ever they do, they can become a nuisance, and even a rival. . . . Which would be intolerable.

Chip's arrival must have been noted. For Dodie was waiting for him in the front hallway. She said, "Chip, can I talk to you for a minute?" She spoke in a low voice.

The youth paused. There was an expression, momentarily, on his face that resisted her attempt to intercept him.

Almost at once, his basic tolerance of the person who was his only acceptable relative, won out over the negation. He made an assenting gesture. He said airily, "What earful has my ever-loving sister got for me tonight?"

Surprisingly, Dodie placed a finger over her lips in a way the Ig had already seen several times. Now, as those other times, the action was followed by a whisper. This time the words were: "There's a girl been waiting all evening to see you."

Whatever it was Chip had expected to hear, that wasn't it. The half-insulting expression with which he normally confronted his sister vanished. He stared at her, wide-eyed, genuinely surprised. "A girl?" he echoed.

Dodie motioned mutely toward the living room.

As the Ig had previously had occasion to notice, Chip was not a person who was ever at a loss for long. Once more, now, his expression changed. The jauntiness he affected under stress was suddenly there in the way his lips twisted into a smile and his eyes brightened. Even the way he held himself changed. He shifted his feet, straightened, and tilted his head.

In that fashion, he walked briskly toward the door of the living room. He crossed the threshold—and paused. "Well," he said aloud, "you!"

The Ig, who had been trailing, at this point also arrived in the living room. And saw who it was that had produced a recognition response in Chip.

Actual recognition did not come instantly to the Slua-Ig. What his perception saw was a girl with long, blonde hair, arrayed in a shining dress. Whoever it was had taken great pains in using makeup. She wore a variety of ornaments: glinting objects that dangled from her ear lobes, gleaming glass and plastic in her hair, large, ring-like pieces of metal around her wrists, and a veritable river of beads flowed over her dress.

The overall effect was a considerable concealment of the basic face and the basic body. But there was also, paradoxically, enhancement of the human female shape. It was a type of overdressed young woman the Ig had seen several times at a distance; never this close up before.

Chip, a satirical smile on his face, walked toward the dazzling visitor. He said in what the alien had come to recognize as a sarcastic tone, "Is the university so hard up for students that it sends out beautiful girls to make sure nobody gets away?"

Understanding, and recognition, came belatedly to the Ig at the mention of the word, university. Of course. This was that girl. The interviewer of the afternoon. Suddenly, through all the artificial things she had done to her body and face, her features took on the familiar appearance of Leslie Bjornsen.

The girl remained seated. But she twisted a little, made a face and changed color right through the makeup. She said finally, "Don't be ridiculous. This is personal."

Personal!

The Slua-Ig was enthralled. Was it possible that he was actually going to be present at the beginning of a human courtship? Data about that, while not mandatory, was desired. Generally, a gameplayer should have complete mating information.

The girl's statement had an effect on Chip. He had been moving toward her in his deliberate way. Her words stopped him, as if she had uttered a command.

He teetered there. His expression changed. The jaunty mood vanished. There was no recognizable thought on his face. Which seemed to indicate that the hard, brittle front he presented to the world had been penetrated.

During that moment, or those moments, he said in a puzzled tone: "Beautiful girl visits space expedition vet in his home—what gives?"

The beautiful girl remained seated, but she made a simple statement—so simple that it must have been thought out in advance. She said, "Will you marry me?"

An ever so faint tremble in her voice, and an accompanying tremulous smile suggested that the words were not easy to speak.

The swiftness of Chip's reaction was amazing. The jauntiness leaped back into view, the barriers, the cynicism. "I should've guessed you'd be a Christian." He shook his head in mock amazement. "Boy, the number of females that got religion the day that civil marriage disappeared."

The glittering apparition in the chair made her first move to get up and failed. She tried again, and succeeded. She said unsteadily, "There's a little restaurant around the corner. I saw it as I drove up. Would you take me there for a cup of coffee?"

"Well!" said Chip, doubtfully.

The girl seemed to brace herself inwardly so she could move outwardly. As she walked toward him, she jingled and clanked softly. "Oh, come on," she said, "break down and celebrate the first time a girl proposed to you. It *is* the first time, isn't it?"

Chip said, "Hey!" And brightened. "Alright," he said.

TWELVE

THE YOUTH and the young woman emerged from the house and came down the porch steps and headed toward the gate.

For the Ig the feeling of enthrallment continued. He thought happily: maybe we can now speed up this whole matter, and get the fleet here faster—his feeling that he needed perhaps just a little more information about the human race had prevented him from encouraging the fleet commander to make a faster approach to earth.

It was another anomaly, of course. In a way even the present fleet arrival time was too soon. (So much to find out, really.) But on the level of taking no chances, it should be much sooner. The Ig decided finally that it would be better to get it over with.

As the young couple went through the gate, the Ig was cheerfully floating at the rear of the neural equipment—Chip's—that was his contact with this planet. Since there was high shrubbery at the gate, and the Ig was the last to emerge onto the street, he was also last to see that a car was pulling up at the curb.

In the car were Mike and Hank and Dave. Chip said to his companion, "Just a minute!" At once, without waiting for a reply, he walked to the car door, peered in the side window where Mike sat, and said in mild surprise: "They let you go?"

"Yep," said Mike, "they were after you."

"Alright." Cheerfully. "See you."

Whereupon, he rejoined the young woman, and they sauntered off down the street. Bare moments later, Hank tumbled out of the driver's side of the car, trotted around to the sidewalk and stared after the retreating couple. As Mike, who had clambered out in a more leisurely fashion, came up beside the older man, Hank said in a blank tone: "And where did *she* come from?"

With that, he turned and ran—into the house and up the stairs, into Chip's room and over to the phone. With fingers that seemed to be shaking he touched out a number.

The sheer speed of Hank's reaction to the presence of a female human being with Chip, had given the Ig the time to hold himself away from the slowly moving Chip, and to pursue Hal's chief henchman. He arrived as Hank was saying in a baffled voice, ". . . I don't know where he could have met her. But here she is with him, as if they know each other."

Hal must have said something reassuring; for Hank's next words were, "Alright, if you feel that you convinced him." After another pause: "Yes, but this one is really gorgeous. I tell you, Hal, I've been with Chip practically day and night. There's no place I can think of he could have met her." Another pause, then resignedly: "But if he doesn't go on that trip tomorrow, I'm going to find out who she is for myself."

As he hung up, then, and turned, he saw what the Ig had, of course, observed just before Hank's final words: that Mike had followed Hank and had entered the room in time to overhear the last sentence.

The man and the black youth looked at each other. Neither seemed especially perturbed. But Mike said, "You sound worried, Hank."

Hank said, "I was born that way. The world never did make sense to me." He broke off: "Chip tell you where he's going?"

"Yeah," said Mike, "over to the Co-op to have some coffee."

"Oh!" began Hank, "the Co-op . . ."

If Hank said more, the Slua-Ig was not in a position to hear it. Because at that precise split-second, the distance between the retreating Chip and himself reached the exact critical point of an elastic stretched to the breaking point. And of course this was not an elastic, and it couldn't break; it could only snap him away, and over to Chip.

Which is where, abruptly, he was.

The girl was saying, "You hit me hard with what you said."

Chip replied, "I didn't mean to upset you. I just said what came."

The girl said, "What I said was a lie. Some of the guys that were killed *are* the best guys that ever were."

Chip replied, "You were making small talk, I know. People do that, not realizing how it was. . . ."

The Ig was not finding it easy to concentrate on the conversation. Wrong things have been happening. That interchange over at house. And the mysterious machine in Hal's basement. The feeling just minutes before, that he had actually been keeping the invasion dead-slow because of a deep-felt need for more information, had been like the opening of a locked door into an entire roomful of additional suspicions.

Still—decided the Ig uneasily—I suppose I can delay my reaction another few minutes—with that thought, and with a conscious effort, he forced himself to concentrate again on Chip and Leslie.

They were sitting at a small table in the Co-op, and Chip was saying, "Now that you're here, and interested in me, do I get a little lovin' out of it?"

The young woman stared at him. "Oh, I'm so sorry you said that." She almost moaned the words.

Chip looked alarmed. "Hey, don't play that crying game again. What did I say?"

"I've been saving myself," said Leslie tearfully, "and until you said what you just said, I thought you were the man." She closed her eyes, and whispered, "I guess you came back too sophisticated for me. I guess—"

At that moment coffee and cake were brought by a live waitress. The girl must have felt the tiny impact as the dishes were set on the table. Her eyes opened. She wiped them with the back of her hand.

Chip commented, "One good thing about these Co-ops, they're operated by live human beings."

"That's why I became a Co-op," said the waitress.

"Well," said Chip tolerantly, "I'm a capitalist, but I prefer Co-op food, and plan to go to a Co-op university."

"I intend to spend my life with one man," said Leslie to the waitress. "Do you?"

"That's the Co-op ethic," said the older woman, and departed.

Leslie said, "I've been hoping to meet a man who

had his mind made up the same way."

"Boy, are you two far gone," said Chip.

He spoke in a dismissing tone. And, as if to emphasize his sudden indifference, picked up his fork and began to devour his cake. He looked up finally, saw that she wasn't eating, and said, "I'm sure glad we've got a few places left that serve old-fashioned cooked food."

The girl reached and picked up her cup, lifted it, and took a sip. Watching her, Chip continued, "I suggest you take a course in psychology, and concentrate on study of character. You sure picked a lemon this time."

She seemed to be recovering, for she smiled faintly. "I don't believe that. I detect underneath all that toughness a tender heart."

"Don't you believe it!" the youth retorted. "I'm down in the mud, with some people looking for me to put me in one of the educational communities."

"You can change your mind any time," Leslie said.

"I sank slowly at first," said Chip, "and then I dived deeper of my own free will, and I'm still going down."

"As you sink, remember a good woman offered you a helping hand, and you rejected it."

"I'll think about it once in a while, and shake my head in astonishment."

Chip completed the demolishment of his piece of cake and, leaning back, saw that she had not yet even touched hers. He pointed at it. "Don't let it dry out," he admonished.

The bejangled head and made-up face had been

staring off to one side, as in a reverie. Now, that head moved to and fro sideways indicating no. The rouged lips parted, and the soprano voice said, "I'm not hungry, thank you."

Chip was outraged. "Just a minute," he said. "All this morality on one level, and total immorality on another."

To whatever distant realms of the mind her reverie had taken her, the sound of his voice with its critical overtones brought her back into the room. When she spoke she sounded puzzled. "How do you mean?"

"I'm going to have to pay for an uneaten cake, which you asked me to order for you."

A faint, faint smile touched the corners of her mouth. "If you can't reason out what happened," she said, "maybe I'm lucky to be rid of you. Here!" She reached over and pushed the cake toward him. "I have a simple solution. You look terribly healthy, though worried. Mother's going to guess that her little boy can eat *two* pieces of cake, and what's more she will pay for both of them."

Chip grinned. "Well," he said, "so long as we finally understand each other."

To the watching and listening Ig, the entire man-woman dialogue had been progressively baffling and at the same time significant. . . . The woman wants the man in a permanent association only, and the man wants the woman in a temporary association only—the two conditions seemed to be unconnected and irreconcilable.

And yet . . .

From his watching position on far Slua, the Ig emitted his race's equivalent of a sigh. And reaffirmed his decision of half an hour earlier: The fleet attack shall take place as soon as the physics of accelerated space flight permits in the confined distances of a sun system.

He promptly did the lateran unity with the fleet commander; and both of them played that game perfectly. The game of the Slua-Ig consisted of putting over the idea that he had solved the final tiny mysteries of the human race totally. And, of course, the fleet commander played his game so perfectly that the alien physicist detected not a single clue as to what that game might be.

"All other things being equal," said the commander, "we shall be there in three days, and home with our families in a hundred."

Games rules forbade asking what those other equal things might be.

The Slua-Ig did not reconnect with Chip. Now that the final decision was activated, the rest of this evening and night on earth, and most likely the rest of the time (three days) that remained to the human race, was unimportant.

The clouds had thickened during the coffee break. Chip stood watching as the lights of Leslie's car receded. The intense starless night made the entire street unusually dark. The corner lights at either end of the block seemed far away and very limited in what they revealed to the eye.

Chip turned away, the smile fading. He thought: I handled that just right. This is no time for me to be encouraging a girl to attach herself to me, emotionally, even though given a little time I could break down that resistance.

But truth was there were things to do. Tomorrow, off on Hal's tour of the rocket bases of the fleet. Then—what?

Blankness!

For God's sake, he thought, is that the whole future? He was frowningly considering what else his future might consist of . . . when a dozen shadowy shapes of men virtually erupted from the pitch darkness of the shrubbery in front of his sister's house.

Chip uttered just one protesting word: "Hey!"

Then strong hands had grabbed him. And sturdy bodies barred him from escaping. Simultaneously, somebody was pressing a cushiony voice-muffling something over his mouth. And somebody else jabbed a needle into his arm.

It was as swift as that. Even as he started to struggle, he could feel the blackness spreading out from his arm, where it had been stabbed, and through his body.

Death? Unconsciousness? He had no time to make his peace with either condition.

THIRTEEN

ON SLUA, the Ig player detached from the viewing, living-in, being-there-on-the-spot, machine. He did his inner muscle stretching, and loped across the room on his four legs.

The sheer stability of himself-in-motion brought a cosy conviction of the perfection of being Ig. These poor humans, he thought, having to balance themselves on two legs, in addition to all their other handicaps, really, they're in a hopelessly complex trap.

And here were the Ig game players, far away from the danger area, safe and unreachable. What a contrast! The ultimate in gamesmanship, whereby you made all the moves, and your opponent didn't even know there was a game in progress. True, the Ig's thought continued, we made a few mistakes. For example, it could have been an error letting the controlled people get away from the earth warships. At first, it was a shock. Almost like a defeat. The Ig fleets were always manned. Thus, no one had thought to include in the universal conditioning of the captured earthmen the idea of staying aboard.

And so, when it arrived in the vicinity of earth, everybody aboard the earth fleet went home. Just like that. Everybody.

After a while, it became apparent that there was no

orderly replacement program—in fact, no replacement program at all—there came a reassessment of the situation. It just could be that it was a good thing. Because there were always a few people like Chip on whom the conditioning didn't take too well. And it was predictable that in an emergency such people might have gained a partial control over the others, and using correct drug therapy, counteract the hypnosis.

Which was, of course, impossible now that the controlled persons were scattered to 30,000 homes.

There remained one enigmatic figure: Hal Steggars. What could Hal do in the time left before the attack? It seemed that he could do nothing.

Still, it was wiser to take no chances.

The alien's first step would be to withdraw, cease continuous observation, get away from it all for a day or so, and then think it all through from a distance. He had already begun to do that.

Next, it was the Ig rule that the game player had to consult a peer group of previously successful players at some time during the final hours of a game. He would have have to explain, describe, analyze, justify—and in the end accept a majority decision on tactics and strategy.

"Really," thought the Ig smugly, "while I'm taking time off from Chip, I can check back through a lesser viewpoint on Hal Steggars. I will do that tomorrow."

The Slua spent most of the equivalent of an earth night having consultations in one-at-time lateran unity dialogues with other Ig players. He was slightly disconcerted when every one of the "experts" stated their belief that he was playing his game with a race that had absolutely no defense against an Ig attack.

The implication was that no particular skill was needed here. The game of defeating earth was one that a stupid player could win as easily as a bright player . . . After all, the very way their entire fleet was captured stands as proof of how simple a race it is. . . .

The Slua-Ig countered the put-down with the mild suggestion that, yes, the anarchistic political system of the human race did indeed make these two-legged beings vulnerable. But that also the system had a number of interesting features. These were too detailed to go into. . . . "But my later full account will be an important, even controversial, contribution to our cumulative knowledge of the various economic and political concepts of alien peoples. . . ."

It was a beautiful ploy; and so he was able to agree blandly with his mentors that never in the long history of Ig extermination of non-Ig races had there been such a helpless, unaware, unthinking species as man.

With that out of the way, each expert, in turn, made his suggestions because, of course, it was unthinkable that they would have no advice for him. So—

He was to make an attempt to exterminate Hal Steggars. It wasn't vital. It wouldn't really matter if that one man could defend himself. But he should try! Also, the psychiatrist should be killed. Again, not vital, but one should be thorough. Finally, and for the end game, locate Chip. And if possible, observe the scenes of planet destruction from his point of view.

The meeting ended with wishes for good luck.

FOURTEEN

THERE IS A way a man has of walking that shows uncertainty. And Mike walked that way as he approached Hal's mansion in broad daylight. In his hesitation was a small feeling he had got from the stocky man that Hal didn't particularly care for blacks; actually he didn't care for anyone, black or otherwise, who made remarks that were critical, or restraining, of what Hal wanted to do. And Mike had been antagonistic.

Still, it was interesting to see the place in daytime. At night the estate had looked flashy—too many bright lights. No doubt there could be practical reasons for that; Mike had the awareness and made the concession mentally. Somehow, Mike believed, Hal was operating in a harmful way; and somehow the Kirlian computers were not able to do anything about it. Also, it would appear from the lights that Hal believed the Kirlian programming could not really protect him. So he was making sure that no one approached the big beautiful expensive house without being highly visible day *and* night.

Mike was wryly amused, having had so many mixed feelings, so many negating thoughts about Hal, to notice a sign as he came to the front door. It said, JUST WALK IN!

Suddenly, he felt a little foolish. He had paused; and now he stood there conscious of how peaceful the world was. He looked around at other stately houses. Rooftops and windows and finely constructed walls peeked at him through trees and shrubbery from beyond walls and fences.

Fantastic. Delightful. Beautiful. Unthreatening. He wondered what he was scared of.

Once again he read the marvellous sign: JUST WALK IN! Involuntarily, he put his hand out and touched the knob. Hesitated. And then voluntarily let go. He actually stepped back. It took him a minute to figure out why he was so nervous. He was, he realized, afraid that Hal was using Chip for some plan and would somehow do infinite damage to anyone who tried to stop him.

Mike blinked, as he contemplated the improbable concept . . . You are an idiot, he told himself. Obviously, no one, not Hal, nor all of Hal's stooges, would; except in an emergency, take the trouble and the risk of violating the universal prohibition against violence.

The tension in him yielded abruptly before the total rationality of his analysis. Freely, he reached and grabbed the knob; turned and pushed. The door swung open upon the glittering, costly interior of the anteroom. As he drew the door shut behind him, he became aware of a murmur of voices from beyond the inner door of the anteroom. There was no additional sign telling him to go forward. But Mike moved now on the strength of the original invitation, and walked through the door and continued to walk despite the mild shock of recognition as he saw who it was that was talking.

Hal's stooges of the night before. *In the same chairs dressed in the same clothes* . . . Was it possible that the four youths had not gone to bed at all? Were still engaged in the same mindless dialogue?

As Mike came up, he heard the one who had been introduced as Henry say in a tense voice, "And then, suddenly, there was a whole gang of the aliens. Just how they got aboard I'll never know, but, boy!..."

Mike thought, irritated: "That isn't the way it was at all! The aliens never got aboard any of the ships. *We landed.*" He suppressed a strong impulse to pause, and correct, and get involved in a heated discussion of the facts. Suppressed it because he was remembering the endless madness of the guys in Chip's back yard. Aloud, he said, "Hi, fellas."

Not one of the four even glanced at him.

"Hal in there?" asked Mike, loudly.

" . . . It's what they did when they had us there cold," said a youth who, the night before, had been introduced as Kosha. Kosha was from the steppes of Asia and had a swarthy skin; so it was difficult to tell from his coloring what he was feeling; Mike had that problem with yellow, red, and white people—there were no visible signals of the inner tensions . . . but Kosha's voice did hold a recognizable note of awe, as he went on: "Those flashing lights shining right into your eyes were scary!"

Mike walked on, shaking his head. As he went through the door, he flung his contempt over his shoulder: "You kids had better get some sleep, and stop dreaming while awake."

If the four heard him, Mike was not aware. Because he didn't look back.

The door he went through clicked shut behind him. It was an odd click that he didn't remember having heard the previous night. Mike stopped, eyes narrowed, and looked around.

He was in the room that contained the bar. To one side—to his left—was a desk that he didn't recall having been there before. Two chairs stood at opposite sides of the desk, facing each other.

The room was brightly lit but unoccupied.

Alright he thought, so the door behind me locked automatically as I came in, and Hal has me trapped in here. An ever so faint sound from ahead and above caused him to glance up at the ceiling. There was an opening ten feet ahead.

Through it a gun barrel pointed at him.

Another sound came from the wall to his right. As Mike quickly glanced in that direction, he saw that a panel had started to slide open. As he watched it slid all the way open, and a submachine gun nosed through it and pointed at him.

Seconds later, there were eight open panels that he could see, and the barrels of eight guns.

Mike said aloud, "Alright, alright, I get the message. I'll be glad to leave if you let me."

There was a faint baritone chuckle from a hidden ceiling speaker. Then the voice of Hal Steggars said, "Mike, go over and sit at the desk in the chair nearest you."

Mike glanced at the indicated chair, looked around once more at the guns that pointed at him; and then deliberately walked over and with a sigh settled into the chair. There was only a momentary delay. Abruptly the door behind the bar table opened and Hal came through it. With the same deliberation he walked to and settled into the chair across from Mike.

Hal said, "You armed, Mike?"

Mike shook his head.

The bearded man said, "Will you reach into your left breast pocket, take out what you find there, and toss it on the carpet to your right?"

As he reached, Mike said, "I don't know what you think this is gonna get you, Hal. . . ." His voice faded suddenly. His hand came out clutching a .38 automatic. His widened eyes glared at the weapon.

"Toss it over there—" The man's incisive voice spoke again—"to your right!"

Mike tossed. After the pistol had made its thudding fall, he said, "How'd'ja plant that on me? What's your game?"

The bearded face continued its steady confrontation with Mike's youthful, cleanshaven countenance. The blue eyes were unwinking. "And now," said Hal, "reach into your right breast pocket, and what you find there slide across the desk to me. Don't look at it! Don't try to figure how to open it!"

What came out this time was a slender plastic container, yellow in color. Mike caught his first glimpse of it when it was already several inches from his breast pocket. And he had a clearer view as he laid it on the table and shoved it over the brown surface.

He said aloud, "You got some smart reverse pickpockets here, Hal. Somebody's pretty sharp at planting stuff in my pockets. And, funny thing, I don't even remember anybody being near me." With his index finger he pointed at the pencil-thin container. "What is it?"

"I'm guessing," said Hal, "it's one of those death sprays. And maybe it's even remote controlled, in which case—" With a flick of the wrist, he tossed the object into a receptacle to *his* right.

"One more thing now," Hal continued, "there's a knife in your right rear pocket. At least it looks like a knife to the scanners."

Mike said, "This is getting to be quite a game. What you tryin' to prove?"

"Take the blade of the knife between your two fingers," commanded Hal, "pull it out of your pocket, and just drop it to the floor behind you. *Don't bring your hand around to the front!*"

When that was done, Hal got up, picked up the knife and the pistol, and tossed them both into the same receptacle at the far side of the room. With that he walked over to the bar and poured himself a drink. He indicated an empty glass. "Have one on me, Mike. And then tell me where've you been, and who's been at you?"

Mike came over, shook his head at the drink, sank onto a bar stool, and said, "I been home. Nobody's been near. Feeling I keep having is somehow you did all this. But I gotta admit—frankly—that doesn't make much sense, since I just got here minutes ago."

He broke off, jerked his thumb in the direction of the four stooges beyond the door. "They get any sleep last night?"

Hal shrugged. "I had a lot of guys over here last night. Who sleeps, who doesn't—none of my business. I keep open house for returned men."

"Yeah," said Mike softly, "I been intendin' to ask you about that. What's an old man of forty like you doing monkeying around with twenty-year-old vets?"

The pink face with its concealing beard pointed straight at him, as Hal said, equally softly, "Let me ask the questions, boy. You're the one who's got the explaining to do. We know what your hypnotized reason was for comin' over here. Somebody's finally got me spotted, and has decided to put me out of business. We need to find out who, and how he got to you."

It was, thought the watching Ig, as good an analysis of the truth as was probably available to a human being. Doing something about it in the time left (less than two days) was not going to be easy even for someone as astute as Hal.

The man was speaking again: "Now, Mike, tell me exactly where you've been and what you've done from the time you left here last night. This time make it a blow by blow account, no gaps."

He listened with narrowed eyes as the black repeated what he had already said but in greater detail. It was a drab story, consisting mostly of eight hours of sleep. However, when it had been repeated, Hal said, "That girl Chip was with, you ever see her before?"

And, of course, Mike could only shake his head, no.

Hal continued, "You talk to Chip this morning."

"Phoned over there," Mike nodded, "but his sister says he didn't come home last night." He added, "I figure he took that female to a motel, or went home with her, or something."

"Let's not have any guesses," said Hal grimly. "We'll check on Chip later depending if he goes with Hank like I asked him to, or doesn't. You and I got a problem to solve, personal, first."

There was a note in his voice, as he spoke, that suggested the solution would not be easy. Mike realized suddenly that his fear was back. This chunky, smooth-faced man radiated threat. Uneasily, Mike remembered what Hal had said the night before, about being able to kill without the Kirlians interfering.

Hal said slowly, "An anarchist society, Mike, has a problem in basic survival. The original anarchists believed that anarchism would naturally have a socialist framework in which everybody joined together in professional or trade unions and that way helped keep things going by agreement. But when anarchism finally came it was a product of extreme rightist individualists and the technologists. The Techs worked out the Kirlian thing, and the rightists set it up so that each person could do as he pleased—except no forcing anybody to do anything. They were quite willing for people to join Co-ops if they wanted to; but don't expect them to join.

"Unfortunately, what it came to is that nobody's really responsible. But the Co-ops sort of got all the soft-hearted types who are kind of against robots and machinery, and support naturalism. The Techs have their own unions, like the Kirlian guardian thing. And the rest of us—the capitalists—provide sixty-five percent of the food and the goods, principally because the farmers chose to keep their land and continue individual work. Same with doctors, accountants, engineers, and bankers. And of course the big stock-owned companies never did stop operating; they merely had special Kirlian stuff installed whereby on their property not only violence but the emotion associated with stealing or destruction of any kind got that Kirlian instant reaction. For them, robots do most of the work, but they do need some human personnel. You work for them, you put up with their requirements, no argument.

"Actually, there's another group, that used to be called bohemians. Maybe they're the real basic anarchists; but even with them some are socialist-oriented, some capitalist, and the rest maybe nihilistic. That last you'll find going down the line of educational communities until they hit their bottom. Most of 'em are not bad guys; they just won't play the game of any establishment."

He paused; and Mike said, "Where do you fit on that scale, Hal?"

He interjected the question softly, as if he were anxious not to interfere with the other's train of thought; as if by sliding it in gently he would evoke a reply before Hal could notice that a reversal had been done on him.

Alas, no luck. At least not immediately. The blue-gray eyes glinted. Hal said earnestly, "Mike, the way it all worked out, nobody really took on the job of guarding the planet—until I did. Twenty years ago, when I was twenty-three, I looked that over, and went around to the big companies. Of course, we had a fleet even then. But since, being a pretty sharp guy, I had the Kirlian thing licked from age eighteen on, I used blackmail and murder to persuade presidents and boards of directors of the big corporations and unions to modernize what we had, and to add new ships until we got our present fleet. It didn't do us any good when the aliens came—what saved us then was pure coincidence, sometimes called luck. But afterwards I was able to convince those same capitalists to tolerate the enforced enlistment of sixteen-year-olds. That was the first mission. Off it went to follow the aliens: and I was aboard more or less in charge. After that expedition came back, I organized another one. And a few years ago, it set out. That one you know about. You were on it. Your old man volunteered you at age sixteen. This time I didn't go. I sent Hank, and stayed behind to see if I could work out some more stuff here.

"This time the aliens were ready for us. They captured everybody, and indoctrinated them all except Hank—whom I had trained—and a few guys like Chip, to a lesser extent, that Hank had spotted as being useful to my purpose."

He stopped. And the listening Ig thought: no doubt about it. This Hal Steggars is the one man we've got to dispose of. . . . It was still impossible to imagine what he could do at this late hour two days before total disaster; but the effort at destruction must be made. Somewhere in all this, there will be a diversion. And that has got to be the moment of death. . . .

At the desk, the bushy face was relaxing. The baritone voice said, "Way you were supposed to come in on the deal, Mike, you were a pal of Chip's. But unfortunately the aliens got you, too. Or you wouldn't have come here today armed, right?"

"Nobody controls me, Hal," he concluded flatly. "And I wasn't here for any purpose 'cause I didn't even know I had that stuff on me. Alright?"

Before Hal could reply, the phone at the end of the desk to his right, made its musical tinkling sound.

And the Ig thought—now, death!

FIFTEEN

DEEP WITHIN THE sleep or unconsciousness state, the individual's identity waits for the light and the sound and the sense of touch—particularly those three—to manifest once more. Then the moment of awakening comes. The senses leap into awareness. Perception of self turns from off to on. The transitional state is bridged in a flash. The eyes flick or flicker open. . . .

Chip saw that he was in a narrow bed in one corner of a small bedroom.

He was remembering by this time; but there seemed to be no immediate additional threat. Except for himself, the room was unoccupied; a quick glance around verified that.

Nonetheless, he did sit up, stretch and yawn. He deduced that an entire night had gone by. Chip dressed lazily—his clothes were in the clothes closet, of all places. There was no hurry, really. Presumably, he had been transported to one of the educational communities. And he was not going anywhere. At least not quickly.

"A man," he said aloud, "who has a little money and can locate the local commissary, should be able to coast along for a time—maybe even for all the time that's left."

As he had that thought, there was, to his mild surprise, a knock on the door. Chip was halfway over to answer it, when a typical Chip Mitchum thought crossed his mind. He stopped short, returned to the narrow bed, and sat down.

"Who is it?" he called.

"Your next door neighbor," a man's voice replied.

Chip lay back on the pillow, and said in a loud but musing tone, "The word 'neighbor' is actually neutral and can refer to a friend or enemy. Which are you?"

"A friend."

"Do I know you?"

"Not yet. But we're two people in the same demoted condition."

"That's a fairly intelligent remark," Chip called out. "It implies that you're an intellectual, which I'm not. May I make a comment?"

"Be my guest."

Chip grinned, but remained lazily on his back. He said, "The demoted condition in which we both find ourselves establishes that we are moral derelicts who cannot be trusted by the society which demoted us."

"So?"

"A segment of this society believes that the careful use of language all by itself, without any help from the Kirlians, is all that anarchism needs. Are you a part of that segment?"

"This is another reference to my use of the word, 'neighbor'?"

"Yes."

"You find that word unsatisfactory?"

"I believe that your use of the word was intended to convey that, since you were my neighbor, you were automatically my friend. I should, accordingly, open my door and let you in without checking into your motives for contacting me.''

''Are you always this difficult?''

''Yes,'' said Chip, truthfully.

''Alright, suppose my motives are destructive. What's to prevent me from lying in wait for you and pouncing on you when you finally emerge?''

''First of all,'' said Chip, ''the notion that one person can all by himself pounce upon a trained fighter like me, and even mention it as a valid prospect, implies several things.''

''Such as?''

''One, you think of yourself as a tough, physically capable guy with build, bulge, and biceps that match those of a small gorilla. Or, two—''

''Yes, two?''

''There are two, or three, or four of you waiting outside my door, all equally tough. So—''

''Okay, so?''

''There's usually a solution to a simple problem. Will you answer one question?''

''Maybe.''

''Are you capitalist or socialist oriented?''

''Neither.''

''Thanks.'' Chip continued, ''What I'll do is lie here for a while and think through all the possibilities of this situation, and then just walk out finally, safe.''

''Alright, neighbor,'' called the voice cheerfully. ''See you later. My name is George Tamper.''

Chip had gotten out of bed. Now, he stood in the center of the room and slowly turned letting the physical universe—the room—impinge on him.

About ten by twelve bed-sitting room. The cot had

the look of being convertible into a settee. Besides the narrow opening into the clothes closet, three doors. One led into a small bathroom with—Chip walked over and looked in—with toilet and shower. He walked back to room center and resumed his deliberate survey. Of the remaining two doors, one of course had been the barrier between himself and the individual who knocked on it.

Chip now made sure it was actually locked. It was. So was door three on the opposite wall, which he tested a minute later.

Back to room center. Survey continuing.

No windows.

Huh!

No matter how long he thought about that—and it was long enough for him to get back on the bed and, while lying down, ponder it there—it remained an enigma. After all, even the grimmest, old-style, pre-anarchistic walled prisons provided small, barred windows for inmates. And this was—he deduced—a "modern" educational community bedroom, suitably—he noted the wall TV, the phone on the bedside table, the refrigerator in one corner, and a couple of computer connections—furnished. Even his "neighbor" had in his part of the dialogue, taken the location for granted.

Alright, so I can't figure out the missing window puzzle on my own. That leaves my special knowledge of the whole Kirlian thing. . . . With a shrug, Chip reached over, picked up the receiver, and touch-contacted a number unknown to the average citizen.

There was a tiny click. Then a voice said, "Your authorization?"

Chip gave his space technical designation—not the variant Hank and he had used to control (that, alas, was canceled) but simply his engineering classification.

The voice said, "What are you doing at Zero Zero 3133?"

Chip was sorely tempted to inquire the location of 003133, but it seemed inadvisable to show ignorance of that information. He said in an even voice, "Checking."

"Proceed!"

"At this moment, how many live human beings are in an adjacent corridor on this level within one hundred yards of this phone?"

"Eight."

"Where located?"

"Four in corridor H-640. Four in corridor H-641."

"Do they have violence intent?"

"Within the frame of a Zero Zero community."

"Call completed," said Chip.

He broke the connection—and made the call again half an hour later. And half an hour after that. On his fourth try, both H-640 and H-641 were clear.

Before unlocking the door, Chip extracted the key from a tiny slot beside the knob. Then he glanced around the room once more, questioningly: "Is there anything I should do, or notice, before I leave?"

What he did was he took three quarters of his money and one item of identification, and put both on the floor in the unlighted clothes closet.

He unlocked the door he had mentally labeled Number One. Stepped through. Pulled the door shut behind him until the lock clicked. Then he bent down and pushed the key into the tiny crack under the door until it was out of sight. Erect again, he noticed a distinct coolness in the air, and a breeze. Which suggested that a door to the outside was open somewhere. To find it, he reasoned, all he need do was head into that small, steady wind.

He headed.

Thirty minutes went by.

He was on corridor H-327, still walking into the chilly breeze, but chastened now, and thinking hard, looking around with intent, searching eyes.

Not much to see. The corridor stretched ahead of him and behind him. What was visible at this moment was not more than 150 feet either way. But such appearances of distance had proved to be an illusion. Several times, as he walked, what had looked to be a dead end, had turned out to be a small angle turn. At which point the corridor number changed.

During the entire thirty minutes he had met only three other people—all men. And the three were strung out, so to speak, at intervals of ten minutes. Chip did not speak to them, or they to him. In fact, each man in turn eyed him warily, and walked past at a slightly speeded up pace. Which was too bad in a way. Chip would have liked to ask questions. But fact was, it meant letting out that he was a newcomer. That was information he didn't want to give up, if he could help it; though, for all he knew, it was obvious to regular dwellers of this Zero Zero community.

Chip had by now decided it was the sleep hour. And that the reason his friendly neighbor, and that neighbor's seven cronies, had ended their siege of his room, was because they were lying fast asleep on their respective cots.

What he was looking for with a growing sense of

disappointment was a hiding place for the money he had left on the floor of the clothes closet in his bedroom. There wasn't one. No slits in the timbers. No nooks. No crannies.

Even more disturbing, he had yet to see an elevator or a stairway. And his hope that he might find a commissary or an assembly room had proved equally fruitless. Quite simply, he was on a level—H—which consisted of a wooden floor, a wooden ceiling that he could touch by standing on his toes, and two wooden walls about six feet apart. In those walls, four paces one from the other—twelve feet, he guessed—were doors like the one that he had opened to come out of his own bedroom. Hundreds of them. If one of those doors opened into, or out to, something other than another bedroom, Chip was not qualified to identify its special quality.

He marked time, then, by running up several side corridors one after the other. Each time he did so he simply found more bedroom doors and what seemed to be more endless corridors. The reason that—each time—he retraced his steps to his original endless hallway was because from it he could return to his own room. And he wasn't sure he could do that if he confused himself with too many side journeys.

The fourth straggler stopped when Chip blocked his way. He was a small man with a bushy mustache and a surprisingly deep baritone voice.

Chip said, "Show me the way out of here."

The little man looked undecided. Then he grinned. "Hey, you're new here!" he said in that strong voice.

It was an amazingly swift insight. And, unfortunately, it was not a good idea—it seemed to Chip—

for him to try to find out how the man could tell. If he pressed for such details, he might inadvertently reveal that he didn't even know where "here" was.

Aloud, he said, "Just point the way, friend! This place confused me from the first minute I got here."

The chunky little fellow grinned again. "Yeah. But, uh, reason most of us are here at all is because we weren't helpful where we came from. So, it's a little late for me to start now. See you."

With that, he stepped past Chip, and started off along the deserted corridor.

No one else came. Four hours went by.

Lights out. Lying on his cot. Moving uneasily. Wide awake.

Presently, a baffled Chip said aloud into the empty darkness of the bedroom, "Have I missed a clue in what has happened to me? Is there something I should have noticed?"

Early in the expedition to the distant alien world of the Ig, he had started expressing his thoughts verbally. *Then* his purpose had been to clarify this thinking on a practical problem aboard ship. *Now,* after a moment of blankness he had the clue.

—Well, I'll be a . . .

It was so simple, so pure, so obvious. After awakening eight hours before, his impression was that he had had an entire night's restful sleep. Yet— there appeared to be no doubt that the sleep period of the dwellers of this educational community was still in progress.

The logic was that he had been transported to a different time zone . . . And back where I came from it's now two or even three o'clock in the afternoon. . . .

It was a mind blowing thought. It changed everything. He sat up, and turned on the light. Then he was at the phone. First, shakily, he pressed the button marked "Collect Call." Next, he touched out the name and adress of Hal Steggars. Since he had to spell out the name, the street address, and the city, and finally spell out his own name, also, it took a while.

Tiny pause. Then—the word, ACCEPTED flashed on the small answer screen. With fingers that trembled, Chip picked up the receiver.

SIXTEEN

COINCIDENCE? No!

It was logical for a trapped Chip Mitchum to try to phone Hal Steggars. (Who else could help him in his captured condition? And who else had shown any awareness of the alien threat?)

Equally logical that the Ig, who had been waiting for something that would divert Hal's attention momentarily, decided the phone call was it. From far Slua he, accordingly, stimulated Mike.

Poor, unknowing Mike leaped to his feet, and dived for the receptacle into which Hal had tossed the weapons. The deadly question seemed to be, would he be able to grab, and use, either the gun, or the knife, or the little plastic tube before Hal could activate one of the wall guns by remote control?

If Hal could, and did, Mike would very likely die instantly. Such a consequence to Mike was, of course, no problem to the Ig. A human being dead or alive—what a total nothing that was on a planet where all human beings would be dead within two days.

Mike was at the receptacle, bending down.

On the phone Hal said, "Chip, what I've been hoping for has happened. You remember what occurred last night? You and I and the psychiatrist were down at that machine."

"The cosmic field thing?"

"Yes. I'm assuming Mike's behavior is evidence

that there was somebody, or an extension of somebody, here with him. I just now had the machine grab whatever it was. The needles reacted, so we've got hold of something."

"What now?" asked Chip. He tried to keep his voice calm, but for some reason he was experiencing sensations in his body, an odd head-to-toe thrill.

"I decided to open the channel between the connection in the machine to whatever it was to your connection in the machine."

"Huh!" A time of blankness, then: "Why not between it and you, or it and that psychiatrist?"

"Because we're here at the controls, Chip, and you're far away. Any sudden kickback won't damage the machine. Now, listen, Chip, hold still for this. I'll talk to Dr. Frith. He has remote control instruments at his home, so he can watch this situation day and night. Do you feel anything unusual?"

"I have that same odd sensation in my head that I had last night, except stronger."

"Then maybe we've really got something." There was a more confident note of triumph in Hal's voice. "One more thing, Chip, that girl you were with last night, who is she?" After Chip had identified Leslie, Hal repeated earnestly, "Listen, Chip, for God's sake hold still for this. I'm doing everything I can to think of ways of getting a crew up there to the ships of the fleet. I swear it's absolutely as vital to me as it is to you that you survive. I'm going to begin by taking care of those Techs that put you where you are, and we'll work out other details later."

"But," objected Chip, "what do I do with the connection?"

"I can't give you any clues. Whoever it is we've

got hold of might be listening in."

"Oh, damn!" said Chip.

"Goodbye for now, Chip."

"I should know where I am—" Chip began.

But Hal had already hung up.

By the time that was done, the violently fumbling, seeking fingers of Mike had pulled back from the receptacle, emptyhanded.

From where he sat, Hal called goodnaturedly, "That's just a hole in the floor, Mike. The knife, and stuff slid down a chute into a steel vault. Better get back here and tell me how you can't believe you're under somebody's control, and then I'll be glad to explain how we control that somebody. . . ."

Theoretically, the alien should now have withdrawn to Slua, advised his counsellors of the new development, and submitted to personal extermination as a safety precaution.

But, of course, the whole history of gameplaying among the Ig didn't include sincere logic like that. In the long ago, in what was called the pre-civilization period, the Ig had played their games against each other. One of the goals, naturally, was to use game skill as a means of better survival and of personal enhancement.

It was all pretty grim and deadly; and only when an Ig genius conceived the game of cooperative extermination of other races did the upper classes abandon the to-the-death games they had played so long among themselves. Only then—everybody agreed—did true Ig civilization become possible.

The Slua-Ig thought with that refusal to delude himself which had always been the characteristic of a good gameplayer: "I admit something inimical may have happened. I shall have to play a skillful game with my mentors and advisers, so that they don't find out that I may be trapped by a restricting force."

As for the restriction itself, that was a problem he would deal with when it manifested in a more concrete and recognizable fashion.

Which, no doubt, it would presently do.

Chip was back on the bed.

On one level, he thought tolerantly, I'm part of a field that reaches halfway across the galaxy. On another I'm locked up in this cruddy room. . . .

Now what?

As he lay there he became aware of a crawling sensation reaching to his two temples and to the center of the back of his head, and inside to the pineal gland. After several minutes more, Chip realized that the tingling extended through an intricate neural network to all his joints—shoulders, hips, knees, ankles, elbows, wrists, fingers, toes—and to some tiny, tiny energizing spot in every organ, including his heart.

Tingle, tingle, from head to toe.

He hoped that it would recede from the forefront of his awareness. While he waited for the damned thing to sink to the sub-awareness level, two half-hour periods went by. At the end of each thirty-minute cycle, Chip made the same phone test as on the "night" before. Each time the computer reported: "Corridors H-640 and H-641 unoccupied."

Everybody still sleeping.

Tingle, tingle, tingle—Boy, Chip thought, this could get unexciting quick!

His third phone test finally brought the hoped-for

response. According to the computer, the two corridors were "now occupied by four persons each."

The sense of relief positively oozed from his pores. He actually felt warm. A jaunty Chip replaced the receiver, jumped to his feet, and charged for the door. This time slip the key under the door in advance, so it would close over it. Then unlock. Pull open. Pull shut after. Start along corridor.

He didn't care who it was. He wanted to see if the Kirlians could, or would, protect him. (The nearest Kirlian extrusion he had observed the night before to be less than two dozen feet from the entrance to his own room.)

Very likely the four men saw him before he saw them. It didn't matter. He wasn't looking. He was making certain he got out of the room, and got the door shut after him. As it was, he made it to a side corridor—and there they were.

Chip stopped virtually in mid-stride, spun to the wall; and then with the solid, flat surface behind him, confronted the four grinning men who had obviously been waiting up the branch hallway. His gaze flicked from person to person, sizing up each in turn. He noted swiftly that they were all men in their late twenties. Three of the four were as big as he. The fourth man towered six feet four, and looked to be a viable 230 pounds plus.

Not that their size threatened him severely. Even here—wherever this "educational" here was—the Kirlians would react to violence that had in it intent to harm. That they had something in mind for him was for sure. But they were—and that seemed equally certain—in no hurry.

One of them, a browned-haired individual with a

pug nose, was the first to speak. "Looks like we've had a dangerous character dropped into our little community," he said lazily.

"Yeah," said the slenderest of the four, a sandy-haired type, "we'd better do something about him before he causes trouble." He also spoke in an un-hurried drawl.

A third man, like the first speaker, was dark-haired, but in addition he sported a scraggly beard. He said simply, "Check, Poochie. Check, Sandy."

The 230 pounder took a step toward Chip, and said, "I think Tamper and I should hold this charac-ter while you two guys search him for anything he has on him that might be dangerous to our happy little haven—happy, that is, until he came."

Chip stared at them fascinated. A fantastic thought had come: Is *this* how Hal gets around the Kirlians, by not being angry? By killing, maybe, for fun? By not being serious when he's around them? Playing it like a game?

Aloud, he said, "I was stripped of all my pocket stuff before I ever got here. I'll be glad to turn the pockets out for you, one by one—so you can see for yourself."

"This guy is really dangerous," said the first brown-haired one—Poochie. "Notice how he words things to fool the Kirlians. He's trying to make it look as if he's the injured party."

"The dirty rat!" snarled brown hair Number Two—Tamper.

"Why don't we all of us move in at once?" said Six Feet Four. "Tamper, you come in from the left front. Sandy, you come along the wall to the right, and Poochie, you move in from the wall to the left."

"Yessir!" said each of the three. "Yes, general."

It was kind of funny. But it was also not funny. Under some circumstances Chip might have just let it happen. Not now.

From where he stood, with his back still pressing the hard wood of the corridor wall, he said urgently, "Listen, fellows, before you do anything, how about hearing my story? I was on the last expedition against the—"

He stopped. He had almost said "the Ig." His eyes widened. His body churned with instant excitement. "For God's sake!" he thought, shaken. "Since I am now connected, could that name have filtered through into my brain? And could it *really* be their name for themselves?" On earth, the enemy had always been called, simply, "the aliens."

And that was, in fact, how, after his perturbed pause, he finished the sentence: ". . . expedition against the aliens."

The first reaction came from Tamper. "Hey," said that individual with the scraggly beard, "maybe this guy's got information that we could use."

The words were uttered in the same tone as the unmistakably joking approach of minutes before. And yet, having spoken them in that dismissing manner, Tamper gestured at his companions commandingly. "Back, fellows! Never let it be said that we operate a drumhead court here. What was it King Henry II said? 'Every man shall have a right to be heard.'"

The other three men seemed to accept the shift of generalship from Six Foot Four to Tamper. Perhaps, they did so because here and there along the visible part of the corridor doors were opening, and men emerging, and some of these actually walked by. Whatever the reason, the four backed off a little, out of the way of the increasing traffic. And stood there as Chip told his story.

He still couldn't tell the truth. Amazingly, the original alien control remained effective. That was the one thing the . . . Ig . . . had really drilled into everybody: *"You cannot speak the truth ever!"*

He tried . . . twice. Each time he felt the muscles in his mouth and throat tighten in the way that he remembered all too well. Both times—the moment that tightening began—he gave up . . . Alright, alright, try again later when there was less urgency—

What he described with interruptions—when men walked by—was his own behavior since his return, including the beatings. His account also included his early control of the Kirlians on the ships of the fleet, and of how that control had extended to the Kirlians on the ground until it was all taken away from him.

"My feeling," he finished finally, frankly, "is, if I could get back up there on one of the spaceships I could do it again, and also could show other guys how to do it."

As he completed his account, there was silence from his hearers. (Men were still walking by, noisily.) The first break was a tentative sound from Poochie. It was as if he were seeking a reaction that his pals might go along with.

"Best story," he muttered, "in the whole community since I got here."

He didn't say when that was.

Six Foot Four protested, "I think my story was better because I came out pure, and he doesn't. He actually admits doing the things that he's here for."

"Yeah—" a puzzled Sandy acknowledged— "that's a switch. Never heard that before from anybody. What do you think, Tamper?"

"I think," drawled Tamper, "we'd better take Chip below to breakfast and then maybe take a trip to one of the fleet ships and see about controlling those Kirlians."

He turned to Chip. "Right?" he asked cheerfully.

The way the words were said had defeat in them for what he badly needed: genuine supporters who would really help him. But there was also in the attitude and manner of the four an acceptance of his physical presence without further threat of forcible restraint.

"This way, Chip!" said Poochie. He pointed.

Without hesitation, Chip turned and walked in the direction indicated. He was aware of the others following close behind. But he did not turn, did not make a single self-protective movement.

They were part of a stream of men. And still doors kept opening, and more men came out to join the procession. They all seemed to know where they were going. That awareness finally brought a thought.

"Before we eat," said Chip, half turning his head, and raising his voice, "let's get out of this building for a minute. I'd like to take a look at the scenery, if you fellows don't mind."

"Building!" said Tamper, involuntarily.

All four men stopped. And Chip, quickly aware that they had done so, paused also, and turned. In a manner of speaking, then, in spite of other men passing by, the four buddies exchanged glances. And then—just like that—Tamper sighed, and sat down on the floor near the wall.

"Boy!" he said, "we're in trouble. All that build-up; and he doesn't even know."

Sandy touched Chip's arm. "C'mon, Chip, I want to show you something."

Chip stood there. He was astounded at their reaction. In a swift series of flash speculations, his mind considered a number of possibilities. But after each ended in a blank as not being an adequate explanation for the response he had gotten, he shrugged, and said in a resigned tone, "Alright, show me!"

"I'll stay here," said Tamper from the floor in an equally resigned voice. "When you get back, tell me the expression on his face. I couldn't bear to look at him myself when he finds out the truth."

The still unnamed Six Foot Four and Poochie Hart also decided to sit it out.

Chip and Sandy thereupon walked silently about fifty feet until they came to a door which had on its panel the number 2211. Although it looked locked, and was to all appearances exactly like all the other doors, when Sandy pushed against it, it swung open. Chip followed the older man into a narrow hallway only inches wider than the door through which they had come, climbed some even narrower wooden steps to a door that opened onto a small alcove with, of all things, a ladder running up to a small, circular hole in the ceiling. The hole had a cover over it.

Sandy climbed to the top of the ladder, pushed at the cover—it tilted up out of sight—revealing what seemed to be a dark, glassed-in room. Except that Chip glimpsed stars in a night sky beyond the glass.

The man climbed through the hole. As Chip climbed after him, Chip called, "Don't tell me we're out in space. What I've seen here so far, all that wood, doesn't have the look of a spaceship interior."

"Keep coming," said Sandy in a resigned tone.

Chip came. And, when he got to his feet, he saw.

Snow! A white wilderness of ice and snow. As far as his gaze could reach into the starlit, moonless darkness.

In his initial, long, visual survey, the snow and ice looked like a foothill scene in any essentially uninhabited mountain area. It was, in effect, night in the low Sierras, the Andes, the Alps. A dark blue wintry sky splattered with stars and—he lowered his gaze—for more than a mile (it seemed) glass-like structures like the one he was in projecting above the ground, separated from each other by a distance of about two hundred yards.

The man beside him seemed to realize his dilemma; for he said in a genuinely sympathetic tone: "Chip, this is Antarctica, in case you're wondering."

"Yeah," said Chip dully, "I was wondering." After a little, he added, "Let's go back down. I want to think about this."

"If you can think your way out of here," was the reply, "in less than four months, that would be a miracle."

Chip was on the ladder now, lowering himself through the hole. "What's the four month gag?" he asked.

"Oh," Sandy shrugged, "the Kirlian computer will listen to your appeal at that time, if you want to make one. If it accepts your story, it may let you up to the next level of educational community."

"What's that?" asked Chip.

"It's in the Sahara desert."

Then this must be the bottom, Chip thought.

That was a wrong evaluation—as it turned out. Worse, the false feeling that there was no lesser place to go made Chip unwary as Sandy and he joined Tamper and company a short time later.

As the two of them approached the group, Chip saw that it now consisted of seven persons. It was not too difficult to deduce that the extra four were the ones who had been waiting to ambush him in that second corridor outside his other door.

Tamper stood up with surprising alacrity. He held up his hand in a dramatic gesture. "Wait!" he commanded Sandy. "Don't tell us how he took it! Wait until we've got some food in us." He turned away. "Let's go, gentlemen!" he said.

Chip was one of a group of men walking along a corridor. Not too many people any more, he noted absently. He was thinking hard yet not sure what he should think about. The outward appearance was that his eight companions accepted him. And there was something vaguely disturbing about that. He kept pushing the uneasiness away because, really, where else could he go, or be? After his long, frustrating night roaming these same corridors, he had decided to get acquainted with the whole place at top speed, and *then* decide what to do. That was what had motivated his coming out this "morning" despite the risk. With a shrug, he reaffirmed the decision once more.

At the moment top speed was walking along a varnished, wooden hallway, again with the feeling that its distances were endless. He did notice that ahead of his little group, other men turned and disappeared through doors, but Tamper and his group continued on and on. Each time they passed a door through which somebody had exited, Chip noted that the number on the door panel ended in—11.

That cheered him. He actually thought of himself as learning the ropes. Suddenly more confident, Chip began to ask questions. The response was immediate. Tamper charged up beside him, and answered each question with what seemed surprising openness.

About twenty-three thousand men lived in Zero Zero 3133.

They were all men.

That was because the capitalist-Christian do-gooders who had built the place refused to pay for a Kirlian in every bedroom.

A Kirlian per room was necessary for the protection of wives and girl friends, who might innocently utter or do some female madness that would evoke instant violence from their outraged male campanions.

But there was a special section on Level G where about 1000 bedrooms did have Kirlians. There each male resident could have a woman visitor once a month.

Everybody was expected to work for a living—in the mines, principally; but also there was seal hunting and fur farming, and fisheries.

"For any of that," said Tamper in a dismissing tone, "you'll have to buy yourself some winter clothes, and then decide what you'll do."

That was as far as the questions and answers got.

The finale came abruptly. "Here we are!" said Tamper. He indicated a door that had on *its* panel the number 10011. It could have been automatic what happened then. The men seemed to all come together around Chip, pressing from each side and from behind him—as Tamper pushed at the selected door.

As the door clicked open, Chip had a glimpse of snow and darkness. A blast of intensely cold air hit his unprotected face and thinly clad body. Involuntarily gasping, he tried to stop, to press back. The next second he was swept forward and out by eight men, out into the snow and the night. The incredibly icy wind froze him numb instantly. He saw from the corner of one frosted eye that there were several other men in heavy furred clothing standing in the snow off to one side. And that just beyond—behind—them was a plasti-glass lift.

The men in the parkas and heavy boots waddled forward swiftly, and grabbed Chip. As they drew him off, Tamper's companions scrambled back through the open door. But Tamper himself trotted beside Chip, and yelled, "Glad to do this little favor for you, Chip! Got you a job your very first day here on a capitalist fishing vessel. You can thank me later. Goodbye for now!"

The only good thing about what happened next was that Chip was pushed into the lift. What was good about that was that it was warm inside.

His kidnappers were crowding in behind him. Chip had time to see there were half a dozen other underdressed prisoners like himself. Then the sliding doors closed. Somebody yelled at the pilot. The machine lifted straight up into the star-spangled night, and presently was hurtling over a fantastic jagged land of snow and ice, with an occasional dark slab of rock poking up from the stark whiteness that otherwise stretched into a murky remoteness.

SEVENTEEN

THE GAME must go on.

Yes, he had suffered a severe reverse. But the Slua-Ig stayed right there in Hal's private bar. He only hoped that he would get another chance to exterminate this incredibly dangerous human being.

If only I understood the anarchistic system a little better. . . . Everybody seemed to respect the system's restrictions. Even Hal Steggars, who had learned to override one or a few of the conditions, remained wary, careful, in fact, respectful.

Maybe that was the real route to his defeat.

As these desperate thoughts ran through the mind of the Ig gameplayer for earth, Hal was turning away from the phone. He spoke again, "Well, Mike," he said, "you've served your purpose. But you're probably too dangerous for me to have you around. So—" with a shrug—"why don't you just go out of my life and stay out?"

Mike was still standing tensely beside the "bin." He said, "Where'd that call from Chip come from?"

"Look, Mike—" The beard was patient and neutral the way beards tended to be even when they were not—"for the next few days, stay away from Chip, from me, from anybody who's trying to do something about these aliens. Just go home and lie down, eh?"

The young black visibly braced himself. His mouth twisted. He scowled. "I don't like your story, Hal. How do I know you're not the advance agent of the aliens? Maybe you came ahead ten years ago to lay the groundwork for the invasion."

"Mike!" Tolerant tone, but firm. "What you think, or whatever the truth is, is not the issue. This is my house—get it?—mine! Bought and paid for from the previous owner. Title is registered with the nearest capitalist listing outfit, and stamped by the Co-ops. My property! I want you to get off it. Clear out! Beat it!"

Mike drew a deep breath. "I guess," he said reluctantly, "I recognize your entitlement. But fact is, I'm worried about going outside where a Kirlian can read me. Maybe the Kirlian won't understand about my carrying those weapons in here without knowing it."

"Anarchistically speaking—" began Hal.

"Alright, so it's my problem." Mike was impatient. "But we're all in this together. Maybe these aliens have been saving Chip and me for the time of the grand slam. You got any advice for me and my problem?"

"While I'm thinking about it," said Hal, "let me walk you to the front door." He stood up, and motioned at Mike. "You go first."

"You got the connecting door locked," protested Mike.

Hal's response was to stride over to the bar, reach behind it, and touch something. He straightened. "It's open," he said. "Just keep ahead of me. And no quick moves!"

They went through the door in that order. And, of course, there off to one side were the four veterans of the recent expedition to Slua-Ig. Hunched up in a tight little group. Leaning toward each other. Intent. Making mumbling sounds.

Mike teetered to a stop as he saw the obsessed four. He jerked his thumb. He said, "You better get those characters outa here, too. Who knows what they got planted in their insides."

Hal had paused at a safe distance. His lips, only partly seeable through the hirsute shrubbery on his face, were twisted in a way that indicated he was thinking. He did not glance at the four. He kept his attention on Mike. He said, "Doc claims he spaded the hidden commands out of these guys. At the key moment, they're supposed to kill everybody in sight. That's all he dug out of him." He nodded, half to himself. "Maybe there's more."

Mike was shuddering. "The average guy'll have mostly members of his own family in line of sight any given moment. Maybe I'd better have myself locked up."

Hal stared from behind that neutral beard of his. He said in an even voice, "Where?"

"I guess you're right," said Mike hoarsely. "No lockups. I been seein' too many old movies." He was perspiring. "You gotta strong chain around here somewhere, Hal?"

"How would that work?"

"I'll chain myself with a padlock, and give the key to my mother."

"Better give it to your old man," said Hal. "That might work."

It was actually a bad moment. The conversation had been too long. The watching Ig on Slua had time to make a mere electronic contact with another machine in a distant location on his planet. The energy, thus released, with its exact coding, he channeled through his own earth connection with Mike. The electronic contact operated at approximately the speed of light, instantaneous enough for planetary distances. The connection with earth had its own interstellar instantness. The two forces combined for an instant attack. It was good gameplaying.

Here in this house was the principal enemy. And, obviously, it was inadvisable to do anything that would have a widespread effect. Accordingly, it would not do to stimulate the hidden commands in all thirty thousand returned earth veterans. Not yet. Not until one more day had gone by. Not until the Ig fleet had made a shambles of the untended earth spaceships. A mass stimulation of returnees would act as an instant warning to all but the dullest human beings.

But—here in this house were these four vets who had had their first stage hypnosis penetrated. They were surely the perfect dupes . . . after the failure with Mike and his weapons.

As the stimulation affected them, the four climbed to their feet.

Mike, seeing them, said, "Hey, look!"

For bare seconds the four seemed uncertain. The next fractional minute, Kosa reached into his breast pocket, brought out a plastic container, broke it in half, and spilled the silvery contents onto the couch where he had been sitting.

The shining stuff burned in the air as it fell, like magnesium. It seethed with fiery, hissing intensity as it tumbled all over the settee. The soft material responded by spurting into flame.

By the time that was happening, the other three youths had run to various corners of the room, and were emptying burning bits of shiny stuff on furniture, on the rugs, on the drapes.

In seconds—literally—the room was alive with fire.

Hal made a yelling sound at that moment; the word he spoke was not clear. Simultaneously, he began to back off, warily, pushing at Mike to get on. He said loudly, "Most of this stuff is fireproof, but even steel burns if the fuel is hot enough."

Mike's reply was not in words. The delighted Ig played the opportunity to control him again. Mike leaped toward the chunky man, grabbing for his arm. He ran into a body and muscles that seemed as hard as stone. Hal's half-drawn pistol came all the way out. He struck the unarmed black youth a single stunning blow with the barrel, enclosed him with one strong arm, and carried him seemingly without effort to the front door; shoved him outside.

Once more back in the room, Hal had his own time of uncertainty. The room was a hell of fire. He watched as, like drunkards, the four arsonists staggered around. They seemed to be seeking an escape route. They needed help. Hal, after a moment's hesitation, started forward to give as much as he could.

"Through that door!" he yelled. He pointed at the hallway that led out to the rear courtyard.

When nobody even glanced at him, or apparently heard, the man moved forward, grabbed the nearest, and half-dragged, half carried him through that door; dumped him and rushed back for one more. This time the heat was almost too much. He made it back into the shelter of the hallway, paused to gasp for breath. And then, grabbing both men by their collars, dragged them along the rest of the corridor, and outside.

The rest was a little vague. He was breathing hard like a man who has swallowed a little too much heat into his lungs, when three capitalist fire trucks and one co-op truck roared up with shrieking sirens. Moments later some men trotted around the corner of the house and helped with the two youths, and helped Hal.

Hal gasped, "There's two more men in there, and there's an underground vault with valuable machinery in it. Don't let the fire burn down that far."

"I'm sure we got here in time!" reassured one of the firemen, as he and his companion led the unwary, unnoticing Hal to the front of the house.

At the instant that he stepped onto the front yard, the Kirlian at the near corner noticed him. What it noticed was a Hal Steggars who for the first time in nearly two decades was reacting to events in a normal human fashion.

In its simple way, it saw the violence he had done over the years. And for just those seconds, there were no barriers to the programming by which the underlying computers operated.

From the street corner, the Kirlian discharged its laser at the man. Hal had a single, horrified moment of realization: "My God, I'll be unconscious for two days—the decisive period."

He muttered the words sleepily. The fireman, who had previously spoken, said, "What did you say, sir?"

But Hal had become a dead weight in the arms of the two men.

The watching Ig had to admit admiringly to himself: . . . A perfect solution to this portion of the game—

Next—Chip!

EIGHTEEN

"SEE THAT seal over there?" said the man who sat at the winch controls in the glass-enclosed cabin on the far side of the big fishing vessel. He spoke over the intercom. He had earlier introduced himself to Chip—also over the intercom. His name was Rogers.

Chip turned from the controls of the second winch—the one that had been assigned to him—and gazed across the poorly lit deck to where Rogers was pointing.

The Ig, who had rejoined Chip a short time before—and was delighted with where he had found him—stared in the same direction.

Chip next glanced toward the ice flow at which the other's hand-finger pointed. Saw the dark object in the middle of the flow. And said, "Yep, I see the seal."

The Ig saw the seal also.

"Seals are stupid," said Rogers. "This is that seal's unlucky day."

"Is it going to be unlucky," Chip asked, "because you have destructive plans for it?"

"No. The seal just saw a killer whale, and didn't put two and two together like it should have."

"Alright," said Chip, "I'll bite. Why would a seal

seeing that killer whale you pointed out to me half a minute ago make this an unlucky day for said seal?"

"Because," answered Rogers, "the killer whale also saw the seal. And he *did* put two and two together. In fact, he estimated the exact distance. And he's now traveling under the ice in that direction. So any second now . . ."

His words trailed off.

All around the seal the ice seemed to explode. There was a great rearing of white, and plumes of snow spurted in every direction. At this distance, and from where Chip was inside a glassed-in cabin, no sound was audible. But at the scene the cracking roar of ice breaking and shattering must have been earsplitting.

Belatedly, violently, the seal reacted. It reared, it turned, it lunged. Simultaneously, from a roil of water that darkened and enveloped the entire center of the ice floe there lifted an enormous bullet head.

Because it was Antarctic night, and because there was a turmoil of water and ice and churning bodies, the ending could only be surmised. But Chip guessed that a killer whale had got himself one more seal for breakfast. Or rather—since many hours had gone by—for lunch.

The wild event, the ice wilderness in which it had run its swift, grisly course, narrowed Chip's thought. Until that moment he had been contemplating with a certain amount of satirical amusement and a certain dismay the fantastic, ridiculous thing that had happened to him.

Shanghai'd, for heaven's sake!

According to Rogers, Tamper and Company were paid one hundred dollars for every person they turned over to Captain Latrille. The latter needed at least fifty men to operate his large combination factory and fishing vessel. The men were paid fifty dollars a day. But the first four days they had to work off their employment fee of one hundred dollars. After that they either negotiated directly with the captain-owner, and either continued on the job, or were returned to the nearest Antarctica educational community.

It was a slick system.

The Kirlians aboard accepted the four-day trial period as not being coercion because money had been paid in advance. And so, for six hours Chip had been, so to say, legally on this ship, operating a winch that controlled one end of a net. Captain Latrille, a thoroughly practical individual, had assigned him the winch because he (Chip) was mechanically qualified, and the previous worker had decided to lay off for a few days.

The net kept filling with small, medium and large creatures. When it was full, Chip and the other winch operator—Rogers—pulled it up with the powered winches and dumped the contents into one or another open hatches on the steel deck. The heaving mass of live stuff in the net would thereupon join an even larger heaving mass in that part of the hold.

Once, while the net was dragging the water, Chip jumped down from the winch seat. He slid open the door of the operator's cabin. Instantly, the cold hit him a shuddering blow; but he was determined. Cautiously, he edged down the ladder to the deck, and made his way toward the nearest hatch. The bitter, icy wind shoved at him without mercy, but presently, holding on with everything he had, he was peering into the hatch at the dead and dying protein-potential, where it bounced and churned below him.

He saw that the catch was being churned forward by a conveyor belt. The belt carried a continuous load of still-live creatures out through a relatively small opening. Through that opening steam wreathed back into the hold.

According to Rogers, the steam came from huge cooking vats operated by other crew members. It was essentially an automatic process. Vat after vat performed either a cleaning or a stripping or a cooking or a packaging process. The overall operation required human guidance. In the sub-sub-zero Antarctic regions robots were not reliable. Machinery was not reliable. And so, reluctantly, entrepreneurs like Latrille used live labor.

The extreme rightists, who had originally forced anarchism upon the world, had claimed that when all the pieces finally fell into place, there would be a survival location for everybody. They were passionately certain that there would not, then, be a single able-bodied person who was not supporting himself.

Even here in this remote part of earth that seemed to be so.

. . . For a while after the killer whale had his tasty meal, Chip grimly compared himself to the seal. He also should have put two and two together. And he hadn't. So here he was, clobbered.

He, of course, was not dead. Not yet. With that realization, the feeling of having been a sad sack victim began to fade. What finally, after all these hours, brought back his basic ebullience, and brought a grin to his face, was a far more positive comparison than the one with the seal. The thought:—How can I convert myself into a killer whale, human version?

No quick method suggested itself.

More time went by. More wriggling small life was captured. The night continued.

And that, Chip told himself, and not the strangeness of the scene, was the real problem. It was the suddenness of what had happened, and of it being night. Also, of the realization that here night lasted all winter. Not only was this, in its summer, the land of the midnight sun, but once the long darkness came it was the land of the noonday night.

The snow and ice visible from his winch cabin on the big fishing vessel wasn't all that weird. They were in a stretch of open water, with ice floes everywhere. The floes were covered with snow, and shone glitteringly in comparison to the black gleamingness of the channels of water.

Not too far away Chip could make out the outline of another vessel, and, beyond that, even more shadowy, a third floating fish factory. According to Rogers there were several hundred big ships harvesting the huge crop of small life that grew in these waters. Because of the physics of convection—the water at the bottom was warmer than at the top—only in the Arctic ocean was there a similar vast catch available.

Approximately thirty percent of the crew consisted of technical people who had been hired at the beginning of the voyage—at some port in Europe, America, Asia, wherever. The remaining seventy percent were temporary labor supplied by educational community 003133; most of them shanghai'd to begin with by types like Tamper and company.

However, workers thus introduced to a way of liveli-
hood in this formidable environment, were thereafter
available, though on an irregular basis. Like the
winch operator Chip had replaced.

(At least, so Rogers—a permanent crewman—
stated.)

In the dark distance off to one side, Chip could see
snowy land rising up to form a shoreline. And it was
there, a short distance inland, that the fleet launch
pad for this area of Antarctica was located. The usual
few hundred bullet-shapes pointed their dark, metallic noses toward the dark, blue sky.

So close. So far away. So useless. Nobody, apparently, even thinking of getting into them and soaring
up to one of the big spaceships.

Sitting there, Chip tried to imagine by what means
he might persuade the alienated men of 003133 to
offer their services to the fleet—now. Not a month
hence, nor a week, but within the next few hours. He
couldn't think of a single persuasive argument.

Presently he gave up on that. So, next, he tried to
imagine an immediate personal purpose he might
have. With that his luck was better. What it quickly
came down to was basic and simple: he was hungry.

Three times, during the long work "day," Chip
had watched a man come up out of a stairwell. As he
gazed across the unlighted deck, the fellow carried
what looked to be food and drink to Rogers.

The "waiter" visibly struggled against the elements. He bent with determination into the wind. He
bravely climbed the ladder to the winch control cabin, the while precariously balancing the precious
cargo he carried. Then, having delivered it, he came
down as carefully as he had come up, and retreated

below. Empty-handed except for a flat tray, which now dragged casually at his side.

Moments later, there was Rogers in his cabin—which *was* lighted—spreading something—dishes?—onto the flat surface in front of him. It certainly looked, then, as if he were eating.

No one brought any food or drink to Chip. He spoke to Rogers about it the first two times. The man ignored his communication. That was temporarily surprising, since he had been quite voluble in connection with their work, and had even been informative about the dirty business of selling men for four days of hard labor for one hundred dollars.

Chip deduced that Rogers was afraid he would have to share his food. Probably, *his* unsocial behavior was an aspect of that part of his personality that had caused the man to volunteer for work in these remote unfriendly waters.

By the time the third meal was delivered, the whole thing was pretty interesting. And Chip was ready.

As the waiter after his third service was edging down from Rogers' high swinging winch cabin, Chip had his door open and down his ladder he went at an accelerated pace. He intercepted the man halfway across the deck, and walked with him to the stairwell. Chip went down the stairs first. (He had found the door locked on the occasion that he had gone down and peered into the hold.) Now, he waited for the waiter to join him. The fellow had a key and seemed to be fumbling with it excessively. But Chip was patient, and wary, and younger by ten years.

"Alright, alright," the man said, as if he were resigned to what was happening.

But as he unlocked the door, he pushed it open, and stepped back with great force. He tried to give Chip a hard shove, with the essentially non-violent purpose of merely knocking him off balance—not an offense that would trigger the Kirlians then or later.

The next second he was charging forward through the opening, and with fine timing thrusting the door shut in an attempt to slam it in Chip's face.

The maneuver never had a chance. Chip was alert, twenty years old, and in fighting trim. He was in with a single gliding twist of his body and by outright muscle power.

The man, a sullen individual with a puffy face, said, "You better go and see Captain Latrille." He pointed along the closed-in deck, "That way."

"I think I'll just stay with you," said Chip cheerfully. "I'm hungry."

"Food has to be authorized," was the curt reply.

"I hereby authorize it," said Chip in his most benign voice.

They were walking along the "deck" now, Chip slightly to the rear—which was where he wanted to be. He was not angry, just very interested in the pattern of treatment meted out to newcomers.

A fishing vessel—any seagoing craft—was almost as mysterious a quantity to Chip as a natural cave. He didn't know the names of anything, or the locations. Could be that the deck arrangements were roughly similar to those of a spaceship. That had certainly been true in the early days of the large spacegoing vessels. However, time came when engineers were genuinely able to think through the requirements of space conditions. At once structure changed.

So now the inner feeling was that he had nothing to depend on except his training, his sturdy body, and his reflexes.

He walked, grimly amused, but damned hungry. Thank God Leslie had offered him her dessert (when was it?) almost one and one-half days ago. The memory evoked for her—from him—a strong feeling of warmth.

The amusing part was his belief that only hours remained before the destruction of the human race. And that, whether it happened or not depended on two individuals: Hal Steggars and himself. Chip couldn't escape the feeling that Hal was also counting on him . . . And I—he thought—am somehow expecting that the anarchistic system will solve the problem if I can reason out a way to use that system here on an isolated vessel at sea somewhere in the Antarctic ocean. The walk began to seem long. At least two hundred feet had receded curvingly behind them. Chip thought, amazed: "For heaven's sake, another Zero Zero type!" These Antarctica people really, really, were a special, alienated breed. Nobody for anybody, except—grinning—what anarchism with its threat of rendering the person unconscious, required from each individual.

He said aloud, tentatively, "According to anarchistic theory, there's a place somewhere on earth where every able-bodied person can live without any restrictions except those of Nature. At such a location, people who are resistant in other places to making any personal effort are finally motivated to try to survive."

They walked on along the enclosed deck. Overhead bulbs shed a dim light for them, so dim that their shadows were scarcely more than flickers of something half seen in a world of other shadows.

"I have the feeling," continued Chip loudly, "that you are trying to help Nature restrict me. That—I should point out to you—is the first step of violence, by anarchistic theory."

The erstwhile waiter seemed to shift at those words. He didn't slow down. He was no friendlier. But something inside him changed; it showed at once in his manner.

Once more he found his voice. "Don't you try to make out," he said in a hoarse, accusing voice, "that I'm causing the trouble here. You're the one that's doing the forcing."

"Anarchistic theory says that no one shall starve if he is willing to work," said Chip in his best sanctimonious tone, "and I have worked, and yet I haven't eaten all day."

"That's your business, not mine."

"True. . . ." And it was. Under rightist anarchism, the person was totally responsible for himself. "But," Chip continued, "you tried to prevent me from getting down onto this deck. And right now it's my belief you're not going where you would normally go after delivering food to Mr. Rogers."

"Where I go is none of your business."

"True."

"And, furthermore," said the man, "no one has the right to follow another person as closely as you're following me. That's harassment."

Pause, while Chip retreated four steps.

He was amazed at himself. Because he had forgotten. His motivation had been so real, and he was so intent on his purpose and had felt so self-justified that, for an indeterminate number of seconds now, he had not given a single thought to the other person's point of view.

And, of course, that was the problem with people. They *were* self-absorbed, and *were* endlessly caught up in justified thought. A special argument might be made for his unique situation; but of course the Kirlians could not be programmed to allow exceptions.

Accordingly, people who . . . carelessly discharged a gun or other weapon, threw anything into another person's face, or, in fact, *at* another human being, dropped anything onto a street from a high window or porch, damaged or broke an object belonging to someone else, dropped trash into a flowing stream, failed to extinguish a campfire, were guilty of arson for any reason. . . . And people who . . . carelessly left lights burning, scrawled graffitti in public places, destroyed a work of art, plagiarized without giving credit, wasted anything—particularly food, clothing, or energy, mistreated a child, mishandled valuable equipment, engaged in vandalism, trespassed on other people's property, etc., etc. . . . got a reaction from a Kirlian.

"You and I," said Chip aloud, "were both operating close to a minor offense; but please note, I've stopped mine. I can't quite remember what the time limit Kirlian programming is on what you're doing, but I'm going to guess that nothing on this level is allowed to go beyond five minutes."

He concluded, "I don't think you'd better continue the emotional state you're in. I have an idea we're right on the edge of that five minutes."

His argument must have been convincing. His unwilling guide stopped abruptly. Stood there within sight of the ship's bow. The man turned—slowly. His expression was a mixture of rage . . . and anxiety. His mouth was working, as if he were swallowing with difficulty. Finally, in a sullen voice, he demanded, "Damn it, what do you want?"

"Why don't you," asked Chip politely, "take me directly to Captain Latrille? Let him try to handle me."

The mouth twisted into a pleased, cunning smile. "Yeah, that ought to be something. Yeah! Let the captain handle a smoothie like you."

Captain Latrille was a laconic looking man, with a lean, very white face, and eyes that were either black or purple. He sat behind a large, antique desk in his cabin, and said, "Really, Mr. . . . ?" He paused, questioningly.

"Mitchum," said Chip obligingly from where he sat in a chair halfway across the room.

The commander-owner gestured politely. "I have it written down," he said, "but it slipped my mind." He went on, "Really, Mr. Mitchum, what and when you eat is something you should have arranged for this morning when you first came aboard."

"You didn't tell me that."

"It's your problem, not mine."

"Anarchistically speaking," acknowledged Chip, "that's true. But there's a related programming that you may have forgotten about."

The lean, white face pointing at him was suddenly grimmer. The hard voice said sharply, "I've been running this ship on a personal responsibility basis for over fifteen years without a single related programming working against what I do."

Chip couldn't help grinning. He had enjoyed his

previous conversation with the "waiter," and this dialogue promised to be even more . . . interesting.

Aloud, he said, with a grin, "Come off it, Captain. You're an early eighteenth century capitalist type without a bone of human compassion in you. Given the chance, you'd be a dealer in slave labor."

The purple-black eyes were steely. "I pay going wages." Curtly. "What's your point? I haven't any time to waste, and you're supposed to be on deck doing your job. Better think about the Kirlian programming in connection with *that*!"

" 'A person,' " quoted Chip, " 'having agreed to be an employee, shall do his assigned job to the best of his ability. Any conscious thought to the contrary, which has an accompanying sly emotion, will, after—' I forget the amount of time allowed for that emotion—'automatically trigger a warning dosage from the nearest Kirlian. A second offense reduces the offender to the first level educational community.' "

Chip smiled, a little grimly now. "Sir, I've done my job all day. The thoughts and feelings I'm having are not those of a slacker. The related programming which protects me from starvation while I'm on a job has to do with conditions of work, and often the Kirlian is not alerted to such conditions until the victim complains verbally, as I am doing now."

"I run a tight ship," was the stiff reply, "modern, with equipment in good shape, no hard labor for anyone. In a wintry climate such as we have here, the automatic machinery is mostly below deck; but it is available."

Chip waited politely until the older man had finished. Then: "But you agree that we have unusual conditions of work."

"And unusual workers with difficult-to-deal-with dispositions. So—" with a shrug—"I'm not responsible for the nature that surrounds the Zero Zero community in which you find yourself nor for the fact that you are in such a community."

Chip persisted, "When my shift is over, I wish to be returned to that community and sleep in my own bedroom there."

There was a distinct pause. The white face had acquired an odd, mottled coloration. Finally: "Do you have any money?" Almost a snarl.

Chip took out his billfold, and waited alertly. "Yes."

"For the meal that I'll have sent up to your winch within fifteen minutes," said Captain Latrille, "the price is $4.50. For the journey back to 003133, the fare—since you'll be going alone—is $28." The commander added, "And that will be $28 again tomorrow morning to bring you back, unless there are other passengers, in which event a refund will be made."

Chip counted out the exact amount, got up, walked over, laid it on the desk, said, "Thank you!" And left the cabin.

NINETEEN

NOW, *THAT*—shuddered the gameplaying Ig with the Slua version of grudging admiration—was a well-played game.

He still had no sense of disaster. Chip had maneuvered himself one tiny step back up the ladder from the bottom of the abyss into which he had been plunged.

The Ig hovered just behind Chip as he climbed out of the lift that had ferried him to 003133. The alien was torn. Having seen what knowledge of the anarchistic system could do—really seen it for the first time—he wanted to learn more. That was one feeling. Unfortunately, it was urgent that he frustrate all further attempts by Chip to escape from the trap he was in. That was the other feeling. And, of course, that one had to win. Tomorrow the fleet arrived.

Tomorrow the fleet arrives—thought Chip, as he walked across the snow and ice. It seemed a completely natural idea. The cold air flowed around and through him, and he thought again that, yes, tomorrow the fleet would come. It even seemed as if that would be a happy moment. In fact, despite the breathtaking cold, he swaggered a little, and was interested in the door of 10011 toward which he was heading. Hadn't really seen it that "morning." It was set into the side of an overhang of rock and snow. That was where the lift had picked him up ten hours ago; and that—the pilot had been adamant—was where they delivered him.

A sadly wiser Chip accepted the adamancy with one proviso: "Your boss paid money for my services for the next three days. So you'd better not leave until you see that I'm safely inside. In case that door is locked, don't leave me outside in these clothes."

The pilot's reply: "None of these outside doors has locks on 'em."

"Wait!" admonished Chip.

"Alright." Resignedly.

With all that precaution going for him, Chip was not surprised when he tugged at the door—and it came silently toward him. He thereupon waved at the pilot without looking around. And then he was inside.

With a gasp, he shoved the door shut behind him. And stood there breathing the warm air, noticing the familiar hallway, and realizing that the interior was no longer a baffling maze going nowhere. Despite having been a pawn, some of the reality of this place had got inside his head.

Chip Mitchum, in brief, had made progress. But now what?

His minor sense of triumph began to dim noticeably. He was a young man in search of a meaningful purpose. But, as he gazed, sobering, along the corridor it was grimly evident that there was, in fact, a great shortage of visible purposes.

There was nobody in sight . . . Still—he told himself—it's got to be different, now that I know where to turn off. Minutes after that reassuring thought, he pushed open the door marked 9011, and gazed along a disappointing vista of corridor. Presumably, it led somewhere more appetizing than had the undoored side hallways of the previous night. But the first look didn't promise any better.

He hurried to 8011. Opening that door revealed the anteroom to an auditorium. There were men standing nearby, two of whom glanced at him as he stepped inside. One of the two came over, and said, "This is a meeting of the Communist Party." He sounded dedicated. "Do you have a card?"

"I'll leave quietly," said super-capitalist Chip, cheerfully. And he promptly backed out.

He remained in a mild state of euphoria all the way to 7011. What stimulated him was the renewed realization that, here at this Zero Zero community, there were some genuine political extremists. He recalled a book that he had *en route* to Slua-Ig (he accepted the casual identification of the enemy as it came up from his lower brain, accepted it without resistance). The entire book had consisted of interviews with various extremist types on their reaction to technological anarchism. The interrogated Communists had taken the attitude that the key to the future was not Kirlian control of violence. The Kirlians—they argued—should be programmed to render unconscious every person who did not share the Communist ideal. The real problem (they maintained) was not violence, but lack of the correct ideal. There was nothing wrong, they said, with violence if it promoted the ideal.

Door 7011 opened onto a stairway going down.

Door 6011 revealed a corridor one hundred or so feet long at the end of which seemed to be an open doorway leading to a large room. Chip deduced that it was large from the sound that came out of it; a rumble of many voices fed back to him through the narrow opening.

Chip walked the one hundred feet rapidly, and peered in at a huge restaurant.

The place was packed. Long lines of men stood at two dozen or more nearby cafeteria-style counters. Each carried his tray, and, in the manner of cafeteria diners, pointed out his wants. The servers on the other side of the counter promptly delivered the desired steaming dish.

Fascinated—for it looked as if he had found the entire "city" of 003133 at dinner—Chip counted the number of men sitting around the table nearest him. He got the surprisingly high figure of ninety. Next, he counted the number of tables going the length of the room, and then the width. 17 x 11 . . . x 90, which came to—phew!—16,830 individuals.

The city of 003133 was eating dinner, and everybody was talking.

That city consisted entirely of men, mostly very young men—mostly not more than a few minutes over age twenty-one, was the appearance.

Not a woman, or girl, was visible, as far as Chip could determine. (Which verified what Tamper had said.)

Abrupt, intense excitement surged. All these men were for this limited number of seconds and moments concentrated in one room.

A colossal thought came: Is there some way that I can talk to all these men, while they're together in this room?—

Enthralled, he walked further into the restaurant;

and in doing so, became aware of an incredible madness: somebody *was* talking to the entire assembly of diners over a speaker system. The voice was loud, droning, and an occasional word was even audible. "This has got to stop . . . The rule is . . . We socialists . . . No further credit can . . ."

At that point, Chip's seeking gaze located the nearest speaker. He trotted forward rapidly, shuddering but determined. It was going to be one of his more horrible moments, but he braced himself. As he came to the long table, with its ninety-odd customers sitting around it on benches, he did the awful thing: stepped onto the bench at a narrow open space between two men—and leaped onto the table.

The diners had put their trays and a portion of their plastic dirty dishes away from themselves and into the center of the table. One of Chip's boots crashed down on three trays. His other foot crushed some plates.

The sound of itself was nothing. Not in that room, with its roar of nearly twenty thousand voices. The trays clattered and slid. The dishes shattered with appropriate plastic cracking noises. The clatter and crunch was so minor an impingement on the ear that not even everyone at *that* table looked up immediately.

It was inadvisable to take time out for guilt. Chip grabbed the plastic grille with his fingers—and twisted it free. It came out, as it was built to do—beautifully—just as the voice coming from it, concluded: "We Co-op volunteers have come down to these Zero communities out of compassion, and we intend to continue to provide these commissary services. But we have an agreement from the Kirlian

Tech volunteers to modify the programming for the purposes that I have just described. As a consequence, certain persons will be required to eat in the special sub-educational community branch D until such time as they are prepared to work. No exceptions.''

During the entire speech, the roar of people talking did not diminish by one decibel, so far as Chip could make out. It could therefore be that only he heard the threat, with its typical sad commentary on human nature, and the proposed solution.

That didn't really matter. During the final seconds, Chip's expert eye was intently examining the direction-set of the micro-processing equipment in the radio system of the speaker.

And he found it.

Standing there, he ignored the diners at his table, who were beginning to react to him. Up and along the line of the indicated set-direction he gazed. And there, far away on the far side of the great room, he saw what looked like a glass-enclosed balcony.

From there—he thought triumphantly.

And took three steps. One to the edge of the table across from the point he had jumped on. One down to the bench between the two startled men there. And then the third step down to the floor. He landed like a man jumping off a moving vehicle. Running.

He raced on without a backward glance. His destination: the glass-enclosed balcony. As he ran, he was thinking, thinking about one problem. The soft voice of the co-op member had failed to get a hearing from this huge audience. How could he do better? The only method he could think of had a human touch, but not an anarchist aspect; and that bothered him. . . .

He began with the four letter words, repeating them over and over with full volume.

In one minute and twelve seconds, by his watch, not exactly dead silence, but almost, reigned. It was enough.

Into what was silence for that room, Chip gave the story he had so hastily concocted. He was a young man in a hurry, because he had an idea that strangers were not normally allowed to take over this little broadcast room. That, after all, was Tech territory.

He was not fast enough. At the exact moment that his thunderous voice fell silent, the door behind him opened, and four men came in.

One of them said, "Come quietly! Or we'll have a Kirlian put you out of commission for a couple of days."

Chip believed every word. And he most earnestly did not want a Kirlian to put him to sleep; though in a way it didn't matter. In a way, he had now done what one man could do in the situation that he was in. In a way there was nothing more for him to do.

But he went. Quietly.

His captors, his guides, his guards—Chip couldn't quite decide how much of a prisoner he was—took him down four floors to a door that had on it the words: SUB-EDUCATIONAL COMMUNITY D.

Chip stopped as he saw the embossed sign. He was aware of the four men also pausing which was a courteous thing for them to do. Naturally, he took instant advantage of what seemed to be socialist softness, and said accusingly, "I heard that message ten minutes ago. This place is for people who won't work."

"And for other recalcitrant types," said the

spokesman of the group of four. He was a fair-haired, somewhat plumpish individual of indeterminate age (as much as thirty-five and as little as twenty-five). His tone was severe, and did not seem to have a single bleeding-heart sob in it.

Chip took his usual swift note of that, and said, "Hey, you're Cap Techs!" (Capitalist technicians.)

"Yeah—" grimly—"and let me tell you we don't appreciate you telling anybody, let alone Zero Zero types, that the fleet is up there without anybody aboard."

"Why don't you Techs go up?" said Chip urgently.

"That's not our job," was the shrugging reply. "Now, get!"

"I work on one of the fishing vessels." Chip made his final protest. "What about that?"

The plump man motioned peremptorily. "Inside!" he commanded. "This is where you eat until further notice."

Chip made one last temporization. "This is bottom, I take it?"

"Yeah."

"On the whole earth, it's impossible to sink any lower than Sub-Education D?"

"Right."

"From here there's no place to go further down the ladder?"

"You got it straight, fellow. And now get in there or we'll carry you in."

An extremely reluctant Chip unhappily pushed the door open, entered—and heard it click shut behind him. When he glanced back a moment later he saw that the men had not come in with him.

For the Ig, it was a moment of triumph. Because

. . . in spite of my mistakes, the economico-political system of this race is so non-survival that the *last* person who had any chance of doing anything to protect the planet, has now been brought to an ultimate dead-end.

It was a moment for another final action. Chip was confined and—temporarily at least—restrained. There would be time to tackle the job of disposing of one more dangerous individual.

Accordingly, the Slua detached from Chip. And attached to Mike.

TWENTY

THE IG HAD Mike in a hospital bed with a bandage around his head. The young black was awake and alert, and in the act of greeting a nurse.

"You religious people have sure been good to me." His tone was grateful. "I'm sorry I can't believe in your junk."

"Oh!" The woman was cheerful. "We'll present you with a bill. And when someday you're ready for our—what was it you said?—junk, we'll take you in."

"How am I?"

"Just a minute." She lifted a plastic board from a rack at the foot of the bed, and studied it. She looked up. "The last doctor examination showed there's no concussion. And if you'll keep the bandage on, you can probably leave tomorrow."

Mike's expression as he contemplated the meaning of her words—it seemed to the Ig—reflected certain thoughts he had had over at Hal's. Before the Ig could make a decision to interfere, Mike said, "I've got a strong impulse to violence. Can you chain me to this bed until the feeling fades?"

"Why—" The blue eyes of the woman widened—"Why, yes, I'm sure. And thank you for being so aware." She went to the door. "I'll get some men."

By the time that was said, the Ig had control; and he had Mike add: "What I'd like brought in here, also, is a phone."

For the Ig, that was why he was here. The phone was the key to his next move. He had no other real purpose with Mike. What or where the young black was when the fleet showed up didn't matter.

A few minutes later, three sturdy male internes arrived. What they brought with them was not a metal chain but a thin rope of an artificial compound tougher than steel, and immensely flexible in the way it was woven.

They took Mike seriously. They tied him to the bed. Around and over the knot they pasted a binding material that could only be removed by the addition of a chemical, which could not be used until they had received a doctor's authorization.

The Ig offered no opposition; made not attempt to detour Mike's reaction, which was: "Good."

A few minutes later, a fourth interne brought the requested phone, plugged it in, and set it on the table at the head end of the hospital cot. Moments after that, Mike—and the Ig—were alone.

The alien prompted the youth to *nis* the signal of Computer Information; whereupon Mike spoke into the mouthpiece the combination of numbers and letters the Ig had seen the previous night on the front of the psychiatrist's automobile, and asked, "What is the name and address of the person who has that license?"

The name was Dr. Alan Frith, and his address 2310 Couch Avenue in the suburb of Milland.

Satisfied, the alien next did the same kind of viewpoint switch from Mike to Dave, and in the same manner, as he had done in shifting from Chip to Mike.

TWENTY-ONE

THE ALIEN'S NEXT MOVE was to get Dave to go to the house of the expert he had met at Hal's. The red-haired youth did not ask himself how he happened to know the address and the name of the psychiatrist. He had left his parents' farm at age sixteen, and had not acquired any real sophistication on the long journey of earth's expeditionary force to and from Slau. Dave's impression: Mike had told him the information the night before; and he took time now to write down both the name and the place while he still remembered them.

On the way he got off one bus to buy a pistol, and got on another bus for the remainder of the journey. His thoughts were simple. No impulse to violence in *his* head. Just a belief that he should ask a few questions on Chip's behalf . . . I may not be Chip's best friend, but I sure got his interests at heart. . . .

The appearance of the house that he presently came to surprised Dave vaguely. But it gave the Ig an instant hope.

Cones. Eight of them. All in a row, joined together, pointing into the sky.

Since the eight cones in sequence was a basic structure for interstellar energy flows, he mentally connected the machine in Hal Steggars' basement to these cones, deduced that the two were, in fact, intricately hooked together—and leaped to a conclusion.

If I can destroy the cones, Hal's machine will lose its power over me!

Dr. Frith heard the doorbell ring, and said to his wife, "Why don't you go down into the shelter? I don't imagine there'll be any problem to us, but still—take no chances."

The auburn beauty (with brains) who was his wife, and who was in accord with her husband's association with Hal Steggars, got up, pecked at his cheek, and headed for the basement stairs.

"My real job," said the man, "will probably be saving the life of the human dupe."

The Ig who had, so to say, "floated" into the house on Dave's extended perception system, arrived in time to see the woman disappear but too late to hear her husband's remark.

Yet the behavior of the two people was disturbing. The alien sighed in the Ig fashion. He was suspicious. Unless I can think of something, he thought, I'm not even going to get my agent inside this place.

At once, he came up with an idea. And so, moments later, as Dr. Frith spoke to Dave through a speaker system, the Slua had Dave say: "Mr. Steggars has been hurt, sir. Chip sent me."

"Just a moment," said the physician.

He had come into a gleaming mahogany hallway, part of one of the two central cones. A few feet from the large, ornate front entrance of the "house" was an equally ornate, polished brown chair. Dr. Frith sat down in the chair, stroked his jaw thoughtfully, and said, "What does Chip want me to do?"

"Sir, when Mr. Steggars' house burned, Mr. Steggars got confused and exposed himself to the Kirlians. So he's out of the picture. What worries Chip is the possible damage to the equipment in Mr. Steggars' basement, and he thinks you and I should go over and find out."

In a small way the Ig enjoyed the dialogue for its game qualities. Unfortunately, the argument was flawed; and so the alien waited unhappily for the psychiatrist to ask the obvious question. It had to do with Dave himself. Why was Dave being used as a messenger? Why hadn't Chip simply phoned?

Pause, while Dr. Frith stared at the floor and seemed to consider the matter. Finally: "Why doesn't Chip go over there himself?"

Triumph. Because it was the wrong thought. Which could mean that the physician's mind had obligingly slid over the right thought.

"Sir," said Dave, "Chip feels that this all may be related to the aliens, and that he'd better not show himself."

Dr. Frith stood up in a decisive way. "I'll be right out," he said. "Meet me at the back of the house, and we'll drive over together."

"Very good, sir!" came Dave's acceptance over the speaker system. Which was, naturally, the only response he could be allowed to make.

But it was still not a promising situation. The suggestion (to go around to the rear of the house) had the look of inadvertent good gameplaying by the psychiatrist. Because, by the time that Dave, on his way around to the back, had walked to the far end of the farthest cone, the distance was too great for the Ig to maintain his connection. Back to Dave he accordingly had to go with no chance for a minute or more to observe what Dr. Frith was doing during that important period of time.

Actually, it didn't matter. The truth was that the alien's game plan to kill the psychiatrist never had a chance. When the physician sat down in the hall chair it was for the purpose of observing electronic responses in a tiny instrument on his wrist.

The instrument was connected to the machine in Hal Steggars' sub-basement; and the responses indicated the same kind of presence as when he had had his face-to-face talk with Chip in that sub-basement. Then he had done nothing. But Hal and he had discussed the matter by phone. They had also analyzed the possible attacks that might be mounted against them. In fact, Dr. Frith had monitored the whole of Hal's experience with Mike, and listened in on the conversation with Chip. And experienced quiet pleasure when he noted (by an instant check-back method) where Chip was.

So, now, the man observed when the *presence* no longer reacted on his dials. He thereupon promptly amplified the power connection in the machine under Hal's house; and as Dave came into focus on the viewers at the rear of the house, Frith shot him with a gas gun anaesthetic.

TWENTY-TWO

CHIP STOOD just inside the room.

The time was only seconds after he had been thrust through the door.

The smell of food wafted to his nostrils. The sights of a cafeteria greeted his eyes.

It was a smaller restaurant by as much as twenty times than the one upstairs on Level H. This one had a single serving counter, and about eighty persons at tables·that—Chip guessed—could seat four hundred.

He took in the solid wood walls and old-fashioned pictures—which were firmly inset into the walls, and mirrors everywhere. They also were built-in, and presumably made of metal, and could not be torn loose, or broken.

Chip remembered that a psychologist had once argued that mirror images were a form of psychotherapy for the alienated.

The argument: very few people were satisfied with what they looked like. And so a quick, unfortunate glance at the awful thing that glanced back at them from a silvered surface constituted what might be called a maintenance system for inferiority complexes. Even—so the reasoning continued—the immense rightness feeling of the person who was against the world as it was, received a small diminishment each time he saw himself.

The builders of Sub D had evidently heard the theory.

Looking around, it seemed to Chip that the proof of the idea was visible. Only a fifth of the tables were occupied. So it looked as if the individuals who ended up here presently decided to go to work.

Chip was glancing over the eighty who had not let themselves be diminished when he noticed something familiar. At the nearest table was a group of men whose backs were toward him. They looked like . . . *Tamper and company!*

He blanked out—these were no thoughts that he remembered afterwards. And only a vague sense of the body movements it took to get him from where he was to where Tamper sat.

The sight of—and then—

Then he had the man by the scruff of his collar, and was twisting him around, and was pulling up on that collar with irresistible strength.

The surprise was undoubtedly total. Yet, as Tamper was literally lifted out of his chair, his eyes rolled up, and sideways in their sockets; and presumably he saw who it was, because he said something.

Chip didn't hear the words. He was shaking, tugging, pushing; nothing deadly, simply outrage expressing itself in unseeing efforts. Unseeing, unthinking, un-grown-up.

He was a child shaking a playmate, and was shrieking something at him—Chip didn't hear what those words were, either.

Somewhere in there, he was grabbed, and held.

Six Foot Four had him from one side, and Sandy from another.

Chip's impression: faces all around him. Men's shoulders, soft with cloth. Brown eyes, gray eyes, blue eyes. Noses breathing on him. And then—

It was over. He was tugged away from his victim, who straightened, and said, "Hey, Chip, hey! Let me help you get some food. And we'll talk."

It was a remarkably sensible statement. Later, it would evoke in Chip the realization that the scraggly bearded one had had previous experience with irate, non-job seekers, who had suddenly found themselves in an unpleasant job.

At the moment, the meaning of the words reached through the fog of Chip's brain, and engaged a tiny portion of his analytical self. Just that small contact was enough to relax the still tense muscles of his fingers, and arms, and legs, and chest. He had been dragged away by force, but still trying to hold on with every ounce of strength. Now, *he* let go, mentally.

And then Tamper had him by the wrist, and was tugging, and saying, "This way!"

Emotion has a flow in it. It moves from state to state in a liquidy tumbling, with passion at every stage. Chip's thought-feeling-passion, as he allowed himself to be led, was a mix. It flowed from rage to shame. To a sense of having done an immature thing. And, finally, ridiculously, to gratitude for the kindness with which he had been handled.

Tamper was chattering. "We had to work fast there, Chip. Could see you were just about far enough gone to cause a later reaction from a Kirlian. But we've headed that off. Which is good—right?"

Somewhere inside, Chip agreed it was "right."

But there was another, more awful thought, also: *What am I doing here? The fleet is coming, for God's sake!*

This was the last night of the human race, and he ought to be spending it with Leslie Bjornsen, the only girl who had ever asked him to marry her.

Odd, how hypnotic that idea was, now. She had spoken the words, and, suddenly, they were in his head like a truth. And suddenly his eyes were watering, and there was a choked-up feeling. Also, he recalled something.

He had noticed a line of phones against one wall, when he first entered the room. Blearily, he noticed them again, and said, "Just a minute, Tamper."

Before the older man could more than turn around, Chip was heading. And then he was at one of the phones, and doing the long distance routine. When the time came for payment of the charges, he said, "Put this against my sister's phone, and tell her I'll pay her when I get back!" He gave that number, and there was, of course, a pause; and then Dodie's uneasy voice came on, and agreed. And then—

In answer to his question, an older woman's voice said, "This is Leslie's mother. Leslie has gone to visit her boy friend, and won't be home tonight. Sorry."

Chip hung up hastily. He had a feeling that if he didn't, he would continue to mumble inchoate confusions from some portion of him that was in shock.

If that girl already had a boy friend, other than Chip Mitchum, then she was the greatest actress in the world.

His brain continued to feel so strange that some other portion of his self paused to make clear that

"that girl" who was meant, was none other than Miss Leslie Bjornsen.

What was so shocking was that her mother seemed to take it for granted that her daughter paid visits to boy friends, and remained with them all night.

Feeling blank, he returned to the counter. And blankly he stood by as Tamper took a tray for him; and he merely followed down the line as Tamper with thumb or finger pointed at entree and salad dishes. There seemed to be a souffle in each of the former, and various green-red-yellow mixes in the latter, in a thin glaze of liquid.

"Some of that . . . and that . . . and that," said Tamper.

As they came to the end of the line, Chip automatically took out his billfold. As he fumbled for cash, he saw that there was no cashier or cash register, nobody with hand out for payment, and no places to put money in slots. Besides, Tamper with the food had not lingered, and was in fact almost back at the table.

Chip followed him, intending to ask about the money, but several hands were helping Scraggly Beard remove the dishes from the tray, and other hands held the chair for Chip. It became a question he would ask later, if he remembered.

Five hours had gone by since his only meal of the day so far. He hadn't really thought about being hungry again. Nevertheless, there was inner space available. He started to fill the space, and once more it was an automatic action, because his amazement at himself was growing moment by moment.

Pressure, he guessed. Too much pressure, too many defeats. And anxiety. After all the earth was about to be destroyed. He had read about the effects of pressure on human beings, but had always scoffed at the idea. Stress, it was called; and when it reached a breaking point, people fell apart.

It was his first moment of uncontrol since childhood. His first fall-apart, ever . . . All those years, he thought, shocked, I built up restraint. And now—in one split-second—the breakthrough—dark, violent, primitive attack feeling. Instantly yielded to.

He grew aware that Tamper was looking at him. The man must have realized that he had Chip's attention, for he said, "Boy, you're a braver man than I was when I first came down here."

The remark seemed absolutely meaningless to Chip. He could feel himself, figuratively, coming up into the light of greater awareness. He said, baffled, "How do you mean?"

"The way you ploughed into that tropical lake fly souffle with the grasshopper sauce on it."

Chip, who had literally paid no attention to his food, stared down at his almost empty plate, and vaguely recalled that one of the entrees had had a slightly oily flavor and a crunchy texture and . . .

"Huh!" he said in horror.

"Good God!" said his table companion, "this is all insect protein. Didn't you know?"

Chip pushed the tray away from him.

Tamper continued happily, "Aguav worm salad, red ant *hors-d'oeuvres*, earth worm pudding, and larva beer—that last from South America."

The tone of the voice penetrated . . . sickeningly.

Chip stared at Tamper; and found a pair of oh, so innocent eyes staring back at him.

He thought: Well, I'll be a . . . He's taken me again. The smooth assistance he had received from Tamper with his dinner while he was in an addled condition paralleled the smooth way he had been handled in the corridor that "morning."

Blithely, skilfully, taken advantage of by a—let's face it—perennial con man.

There was no problem of understanding. Everybody knew about insect food. It was free. Cashiers were not required. This was capitalist welfare in an anarchist state. Nothing wrong with insect protein, scientists agreed. As good as shrimp, or fish, or animal meat. But for some reason most people of West European-American origin thought about that for about two seconds, and decided maybe work was better. (In central Africa, would-be laggards had the same reaction to shrimp and other shellfish. And that, of course, was what *they* were threatened with. And reacted to.)

Except, of course, for a few who refused to be affected.

There were always those few. Everywhere. Their alienation reported in earliest recorded history.

And most of those few, it had been repeatedly observed from the most ancient times, would work if the alternative was the lash.

But they didn't change their minds. They weren't re-educated. They just played your game—and hated you every minute. And waited for an opportunity.

TWENTY-THREE

SOMEWHERE IN THERE Chip recovered. It was his
old method. If pressure let up at all, he bounced. He
couldn't help it. Suddenly, the grin. The steep rise in
spirits. The feeling of got-to-take-life-as-it-is.

He made no attempt to finish the tiny amount of
substance left on his plate. But the momentary emotional response that had almost caused him to bring
up what he had eaten receded to that distant location
where stomach cramps go when they no longer
cramp. Presumably, his digestive system would in
due time dispose of the hordes of insects he had
swallowed.

He grew aware that a thought was trying to form in
his mind, seeking an opportunity to express itself.
The opportunity came, and Chip said to Tamper, "I
took it for granted that you and your friends would by
this time be up on one of the fleet ships."

As he spoke the words, he realized that he was
actually intensely disappointed that they weren't.
*And that that disappointment had flashed through
him at the exact instant that he first saw Tamper*.

It could even be—it occurred to him belatedly—
that their failure to go was what, in fact, had triggered
his wild, desperate attack.

Thinking about it, consciously now, he experienced an inner crunch feeling.

And realized that he was back to the real basic of this whole drab, deadly situation: getting somebody to man the fleet.

Tamper was speaking, "I got a business here to attend to. I can't be taking vacations on impulse."

"A business!" echoed Chip, nonplussed. Somehow, he hadn't thought of the older man's activities in precisely that term.

"I run an employment agency," Tamper went on, "and that's a very specialized thing in Antarctica."

"I can guess," said Chip, ironically, and completely cheerful again. "What puzzles me is how come a business man is on welfare?" He motioned vaguely at his own plate with its small amount of leftovers.

"Well," said the man, "the way that works is that they don't approve of my business here, and there's no place else to put me." His brown eyes twinkled with the amusement of the man who has finally beat all the games of the establishment. "Sub-educational Community D is bottom." He shrugged. "I figured if my stomach will digest the stuff, then I got no problem. Fact is—" he confided—"I'm beginning to think it tastes good. Maybe it's going to turn out that at some future time this is what the real gourmets eat."

Small pause, while Chip considered that, in a peculiar way, he also was letting his stomach handle the problem of about eight thousand insects. Interesting that both Tamper's and his own automatic solution had been, in a manner of speaking, to sit back and live a separate existence from their digestive tracts. He said finally, "Did you hear my speech over the—?" With his right thumb he motioned toward the speaker box which, here also, hung down from the ceiling above the center of the long table.

"Hey, was that you? I didn't recognize your voice. Besides, I thought you were at—" Tamper stopped.

Chip could not suppress a grin at the almost-slip. No question about where Tamper had believed Chip Mitchum would be: in a tiny bunk aboard a floating cannery, in a dark icy sea, offshore from a fantastic frozen wasteland.

"Think anybody'll go?" Chip asked, striving hard to keep his voice neutral.

"Are you kidding? Hey, Sandy!" The lean, brown-haired Tamper turned to glance along the table towards where his companion sat. "What you getting on that migration?"

The blond haired one ceased talking to *his* table companion, and glanced down at something—a tiny instrument of some kind—lying on the table beside his plate. "Hmmm!" he said. "The computer that monitors all exits says 122, and it's . . ." He paused, and glanced at his watch and then at the instrument, back and forth several times—"it's adding on four every ten seconds. Looks like a good response." A grin. "The fleet is about to have the experience of its career, hey!"

To Chip, Tamper said matter-of-factly, "Looks like that three days of good food with pay, and a change of climate, has got its own appeal. Ought to be quite a crowd up there by noon tomorrow." He added, "It's only about a mile and a half walk to the takeoff pad; and so I'm guessing these first guys rushed to their room, dressed in their warm clothing, and left."

Chip said aloud, disappointed. "Only a hundred

and twenty-two." He added in a hopeless tone, "Maybe the slower ones will all leave together in one big swoosh in the next couple of hours or so."

"Maybe eight hundred all together," said Tamper. He pursed his lips. "What's all this eagerness to get these lamebrains up to wreck the fleet? You got a grudge?"

"Eight hundred!" echoed Chip.

The estimate was so far below what was needed that he felt himself shrinking. He said vaguely, "What I don't understand, if she's so pure how come her mother casually accepted her going out for the—?"

"Huh!" interjected Tamper at that point.

Chip was on his feet. His eyes were wide and staring. "Hey, maybe she's coming *here*?"

"Who?"

The question was directed toward a temporarily deranged mind. "Is there some way to get out of this place?" Chip yelled.

"The doors opened ten minutes ago, and—" Shrewdly—"the location of that thousand room love nest is Level G, North."

TWENTY-FOUR

SHE WAS WAITING for him in what was called the Lover's Lounge. Dressed in slacks, her long blond hair straggling to her shoulders, wrapped in a mock-fur coat, wearing not a single item of jewelry, she sat curled up on a settee. And had evidently been there for quite a while. The packsack beside her looked slept on.

"You'll be needing a woman while you're here!" was her wan-voiced greeting, as Chip came up. Tamper and company had paused in the doorway, and she evidently did not connect them with him.

There was a pause. All the running and walking had exhausted most of the madness out of Chip. Suddenly, he was thinking about what he ought to be doing. He ought to be up in one of the ships.

"How did you find out I was here?"

"A friend of yours—a Dr. Alan Frith—called me."

"Who?"

"He's a psychiatrist."

Chip was bemused . . . So now I find out his name—He was about to let the information be just that, when a whole series of realizations about the improbabilities involved, hit him.

"Just one minute," he said. He saw that the girl

was looking at him, puzzled. Chip said reassuringly, "Don't mind me! I'm beginning to get a picture of a prime mover doing some moving. "The way I see this now," Chip continued, "is Dr. Alan Frith, earthside gameplayer. I'm betting he's the one that had those Techs strip me of my connection with the Kirlians, and then had them bring me down here where I'd be out of the way. No direct break with Hal, his hatchet man. Just make sure that Hal and his cronies—meaning Hank and me—don't interfere with the game. Even sending you down to see me could be one more way of keeping me occupied during a key time. The implication is: don't rock the boat because the game is in earth's favor. Well—" Cynically—"he's safe. I haven't been able to do a thing."

The girl said in a beaten voice, "You want me to go?"

And, of course, that was not the idea. He walked over and sank down beside her. She uncurled, and fell toward him.

It was total surrender. Warmth. Agreement. Interest. Acceptance.

Chip said, "I'll see if I can rent a room."

"I've already rented one."

"Okay." He got up, excited; but not entirely happy. Like a warrior of old, the battle was first, the woman second. The defense of the realm must take precedence over the joys of domesticity.

Leslie seemed to be unaware of his mixed reaction. Because, when he leaned down to take her hands with the intent of pulling her to her feet, she came up and into his arms with an easy, gliding movement.

At that exact instant in faraway America, Dr. Alan

Frith turned up the power on the machine in Hal's sub-basement.

"Good God!" said Tamper, who had walked farther into the room. "Look at him!"

To Chip, the voice sounded faraway. Almost unnoticing, he let go of Leslie, and turned questioningly toward the group of men. They had all come forward, and were standing a dozen feet away staring at him.

He said to Tamper, "Look at whom?"

His own voice made a hollow effect in his ears, as if he were listening through a tunnel.

"You!" said the man in a voice that was suddenly a tiny, faraway echo as from a child's toy. "Take a look in one of those mirrors!"

He was walking, and his legs felt gummy. Or—no—it was more as if he were at the bottom of a pool, and the water dragged against him as he tried to move. Yet, since he had a near destination—a wall mirror—there he was, presently, staring at the reflection of himself that stared back at him.

What he saw . . . was . . .

The eight men and the young woman who were watching him, saw him stagger, and sink to the floor. Leslie uttered a cry, ran over, and kneeling beside him, said, "Chip! Chip!"

As she knelt there beside the collasped body, Tamper whispered to Sandy and Six Foot Four, who were nearest him: "Seems a shame. There's that poor girl all warmed up. She really shouldn't have to go to bed tonight by herself."

"Still," Sandy whispered back, "Chip's a real man. It would take all eight of us to be a substitute for him."

"But—" protested Six Foot Four—"isn't that against Kirlian programming? Won't there be penalties?"

Tamper rolled his eyes sanctimoniously. "When you're going to do a good deed for somebody, you can't think of yourself. Besides, the penalty is living in a Zero Zero educational community and eating in Sub D. Surely, for a worthy cause . . . "

Moments after that he was kneeling beside Leslie. "Look, kid," he said in his gentlest con voice, "we're Chip's pals. I think we should carry him down to Level A where the hospital is."

"Oh, would you, please?"

"Maybe you'd better come down there and be his nurse."

The girl looked up, tears in her eyes. "Oh, they won't let me out of this area," she sobbed. "That Co-op volunteer who sits at the barrier said it was forbidden."

"You want to go down there," said Tamper, "we'll get you there. For a pal, we'll take the chance."

"For God's sake," Leslie mumbled through her crying, "what could have happened? Look at him! He's all lit up. We've got to get him to a doctor."

"Just leave it all to us," soothed good old George Tamper.

He turned and looked up at his cronies. Six Foot Four and the second largest of the group he directed to carry Chip. To the remaining six, he said loud and clear, "Gentlemen, we're going to have to ask two of you to make a small sacrifice for this young lady and her lover, our friend Chip. As we come up to the barrier, you Dessar and you Planchette, grab the guy on duty, and hold him. If you hold the right thoughts it could be that there'll be no Kirlian reaction at all. Usually, for just holding somebody against his will, if you don't intend harm to him—which you don't— there's no Kirlian kickback for five minutes. But even then you only get a ten minute dose of unconsciousness. Which isn't too bad, considering what your intentions are. Right?''

It seemed to be all right.

TWENTY-FIVE

THE IG, AT the moment when the connection was intensified between himself and Chip, withdrew to Slua. Uneasily, because the threat was personal, he trotted out onto the balcony of his science room. It was relaxing and pleasurable to survey his domain. He saw first, the courtyard of his baronial palace which had the usual appearance of busy Ig servants and lower classes doing their jobs.

Beyond that, the military garrison, and the air and space ports swarmed with the activity of the uniformed guards, and the glitter of the small craft that patrolled his province was an almost ceaseless movement in the sky.

And then, in the distance to the farthest horizon, his capitol city spread. Seen from the battlements of his balcony, it seemed almost visionary in its gleaming beauty; from here there was no sign that many of the buildings had been transported from planets, the inhabitants of which had been destroyed to the last individual. And that in fact his province was swollen with the spoils of extermination.

The Slua did a swift touching of minds with the captain of the garrison, the commander of the airport and the supreme of the spaceport. Presumably, they also played their games with him, but his end of the contact was a precise limited interchange that evoked from each of the three the exact reassuring subservience of the middle ranks of Ig society. The Great Baron informed in his best Upper Level manner that he wished to be brought up to date on the state of control that it had been necessary to exercise during his gameplaying absence.

"Just a couple of minor incidents, Noble Sir. The usual youthful ungrateful types. We executed two of the ring leaders, and dispersed the rest. No problem."

"Very good."

Thereupon, the galactic gameplayer—only the Ig nobility was given the training and the privilege of playing the interstellar game of destruction—went back into his special room, and *nis*-ed for a family gathering.

A few minutes later, as he entered the great audience chamber two floors down, it was evident that everybody had instantly ceased doing whatever was personal to each—had ceased that and had rushed to be with the Great Ig.

Well, almost everybody. As his nine wives paraded past him in the traditional bent-over position, three did the ritual apology for the absence of an offspring. In each instance the missing offender was engaged upon an acceptable duty.

The Slua invited Wife Number Four to have food prepared in her chamber. He would visit her there later for a limited time. She acknowledged the honor, as befitted a well-trained wife, by falling at his feet; from which position he stooped and graciously raised her.

When he presently, after about eight earth hours, returned to the science room, he wasted no time, but tuned in the viewer-contact at once.

TWENTY-SIX

THE IG found the body of Chip lying on the floor of the restaurant of Sub-Education D. The young human being was either asleep or unconscious. His breath came slowly and evenly.

All around, emptiness. No sound. No movement. The long dining tables were deserted, and there was no one standing in line at the serving counter, and nobody and no food behind the counter.

A dozen or so drab minutes went by. And then—a distant door opened. In single file Tamper and his seven associates entered. They walked over to Chip, and stared down at him. One of the men said, "For God's sake, he's still out!"

The simple words that had been spoken by the Tamper seemed to be a signal that somebody had been waiting for. A man's voice said urgently, "Chip, are you awake?"

Tamper walked forward, and stood above the unresponsive body on the floor. A puzzled expression was on his face.

"Hey, Chip—" The voice came again—"answer me!"

Scraggly Beard noticed this time that the voice came from the area of Chip's collar. He bent lower, and said, "Whoever you are, if you can hear me, I'm a friend of Chip's. He's lying here, and has now been either asleep or unconscious an entire sleep period. Where are you sending from?"

"I'm Hank Swain. I landed at the jet port here half an hour ago. How do I get to where Chip is?"

Tamper said, "Can you do him any good?"

"I have Dr. Frith with me," was the reply. "He knows what the problem is. In fact, that's why he's here: to help Chip."

"What is the problem?"

There was a pause. Then another voice said, "Chip is going through the sleep stage of being connected to a special consciousness expansion machine. He should awaken soon, but when he does he'll need some guidance."

"Wel-l-l-ll!" said Tamper.

Suddenly, the con-man gleam was in his eyes. He motioned at Six Foot Four and the man—Dessar—next to him. The two men bent their heads towards him.

Tamper whispered, "Strip him to his shorts. His clothes have that special radio system woven into them. We can use that."

As this was being done—roughly and hurriedly—Tamper again bent forward, and said aloud, "Do you have Chip's room number?"

"Yes," said Hank's voice.

"Have somebody direct you over. No, wait!—" Glibly. "We'll come over and get you. Tamper is my name."

He whispered to Sandy: "Contact Helicopter Service. Tell 'em we've got a couple of employees for one of our special customers."

"Right!" said Sandy, shaking his head admiringly.

The way they worked the theft of Chip's clothing was simple con. The two men who had stripped him handed the suit over to Poochie, as Tamper whispered: "Mr. Hart, take these to a suitable Co-op Lost and Found department."

Kirlians could be deceived by such tactics. The clothing could be transported an indefinite distance so long as Poochie held the right thought. Which, under normal circumstances, he was qualified to do.

Swiftly, now, again in single file, the seven who remained after the departure of Poochie, also exited.

The distant door opened. And closed.

Once more, emptiness, silence.

Time passed silently. But—suddenly—a sound! Pots and pans clattered from a point to the left of Chip's inert body. Presently, it became apparent that the cook had entered the kitchen of Sub-D.

More time went by.

The sounds in the kitchen continued. There were several people now; several voices chatting in muffled tones. Then—something slammed against something.

The clattering noise came into the restaurant in the form of a wheeled vehicle that rolled over to the serving counter. Whereupon, two men lifted large pots, which they lowered into various containers in the counter. The job done, they returned to the kitchen with their wheeled vehicle.

During the moments when the swinging door was open, one of the two called to whoever was inside: "Better not make too much of that junk. Nobody out here yet."

Seconds after that his final statement was proved a lie. The distant corridor door opened with a crash, and three customers entered. They all walked by where Chip lay on the floor, glanced at the still body, and walked on.

Other men began to arrive. Finally, the twenty-third of these said casually to one of the behind-the-counter servers, "There's a stiff lying over here against the wall. Looks like he's been rolled."

After about five minutes, a Co-op medical emergency squad entered. They wheeled Chip out the corridor door on a powered dolly, down an elevator to Level A, and so to a hospital bed.

A young Cap doctor—all doctors were capitalists—examined the still-breathing body, frowned, brought a machine over and, after a while, said, "He'll be all right. He's got an expanded consciousness thing going, and will awaken eventually."

He turned to the squad, meticulously addressed them as if they were all equals:

"The proper thing to do would be to take him back where you got him. But, failing that, I'd appreciate if if you'd carry him to the nearest hallway, and dump him there."

One of the Co-ops, evidently a bleeding-heart type, said shocked: "Why not leave him in the bed here until he awakens? We'll have to make up this bed anyway; so he might as well stay in it a while."

The Cap Doc shook his head. "Whoever this is, did this to himself, or had it done to him—since it would be illegal to connect him to such a machine without his permission. We're in the same spot. We can't take responsibility for him unless he's a casualty. If he wants to play around with images of the early history of the cells, that's his business. There's a programming in the Kirlians about interfering with an individual's responsibility for therapy of any kind."

The Co-op made one more protest: "He looks as if he's been rolled. Maybe we could put him into that pair of pants hanging in the storeroom, and the sweater that's been stashed in one corner of the lab the last six months."

"Suit yourself," said the Medic, turning away, indifferently.

Less than ten minutes later, Chip's body was again lying near the wall in the restaurant of Sub-D.

TWENTY-SEVEN

SO FAR so good.

The Ig contacted the fleet commander, and heard good news: "Your excellency, we have just arrived in the vicinity of earth, and everybody is at battle stations."

"Anything I should know?" asked the Great Ig.

"Eleven of the earth ships have left their orbits, and seem to have gone off on eleven separate courses."

The Slua was puzzled. "Did they see you, and depart?"

"No. According to the spy instruments we put aboard when we originally captured these vessels, each ship has about a hundred men on it. The appearance is that they just decided to go off somewhere. This is acutally in our favor."

"How so?"

"On the remote chance that the destruct systems we put aboard were discovered—their departure means that if people on the planet below become alarmed and try to join the fleet, well, it just isn't there.

"What about the other four?"

"The men aboard those craft seem to be absorbed in the small human type amusements available on all these vessels."

"What do you intend to do?"

"Proceed according to plan. We're all eager to get this over with, and come home. May I disconnect, sir?"

Disconnection was permitted.

The Ig game player was content. There lay the unconscious body of Chip. Hank and Dr. Frith were being taken care of. Hal Steggars was unconsious in a remote hospital. The earth fleet was gone, taken off somewhere by earth's most alienated anti-anything males. And the four vessels that remained in orbit were undoubtedly signalling the presence of strange ships; but nobody was listening.

True—acknowledged the Slua-Ig—I'm still attached to Chip through Hal's machine. But that connection will end when the massive destruction wipes out the machine, and a short time later wipes out Chip himself.

As things stand, Chip will, for a short time, be able to watch the end of his planet through me.

"Human society," thought the Slua, "resembles the universe itself, in that there is no government. The universe is in a colossal anarchistic condition. Its different elements interact. Some of the elements survive. Many succumb. But no central intelligence such as a government decides which shall be favored and which not. A system like that on a vast intergalactic scale makes sense. It is objective, unconcerned with individuals or groups. A planet is too small a stage for such an idea. So, I predict that the human race, which had the temerity to try to imitate the structure of the universe itself, will cease to exist within a few hours.

"The game is accordingly won."

TWENTY-EIGHT

. . . . A STEADY, faint, musical clicking, with, each
time, faint harmonics. A sense of . . . distances.
Many distances. As if echoes were coming back to
him from an endless number of locations.

Pictures of flowers, in color, floated through his
brain. Each flower had its mirror image, which had
its mirror image—an actual visualization of endless
images going back and back in some inner vista of the
mind.

And with every musical click and every flower—a
thought.

A million million million thoughts.

How can the human brain make sense out of that
much information?

It wasn't quite like that. All life is confronted instant by instant through its perception centers by
millions upon millions of separate data. In a single
glance of 180° the human eye embraces half the sky
and half the visible earth to the horizon. But what the
brain really takes note of is a selected focal point
involving a few billion light rays only.

More important—when Chip was originally connected to the Kirlian system, his brain had a pattern
imposed on it. The pattern duplicated every bubble,
every charged packet of molecules, and even every

energy flow in the Kirlian network. . . .

It was apparent that he was coming to. Whatever the time was that the doctor had had in mind when he said that there would eventually be an awakening—that time had passed.

The outward appearance of the awakening: the youthful body on the floor groaned several times. And stirred. Then the eyes flickered, and opened. A pause. But, finally, Chip sat up and tried to look around.

He was not yet aware of his immediate surroundings. He seemed to be three people, three thought centers, somehow intertwined. An added confusion: one of the three was not human. The other thought center was Dr. Alan Frith.

Even as Chip recognized who it was, the music inside him changed slightly—and one of the flowers stopped moving, flickered, and dissolved into a faint caricature of an outline of human male figure. Swiftly, the outline moved into sharper focus. It became a ghostly version of the psychiatrist.

"Hi, Chip," said this apparition. It sounded like Frith's voice.

"Where are you?" asked Chip. He seemed to speak the words aloud.

"Does it matter?" A grin. "But the answer is, everywhere. Just like you."

"That's what I don't understand," Chip complained. "I thought I was disconnected from the Kirlian circuit."

"Well, Chip, I had the problem of fooling a being whose abilities at the beginning were an unknown quantity. You may recall that I said we probably understand hypnotism better than they do."

"I recall, sir. I don't see how it applies to me. I *was* disconnected. Some very determined Tech A's disconnected me."

"It's nice," smiled the ghostly Dr. Frith, "to have people who believe in what they're doing. But Techs in our anarchistic society are the closest to being in a position of power of any of the unions. Their job is to keep the Kirlians working. Thus they're a lower level version of chief aides to a king. And it shows in their behavior, which constantly borders on the aggressive. Observing this, the other science unions have an understanding that they will not share their special knowledge. As a result the Techs don't know what I know about manipulating the Kirlians. Their arrogance—which is not their fault as individuals; it's just the way people are—has reduced them to the level of maintenance mechanics while, of course, they think they're engineers. Too bad—but it puts you back in power. Yet you were basically never really out of it. All right?"

"I felt out—until this started: these flowers."

The psychiatrist's voice continued earnestly, "Chip, a pattern was impressed on your brain when Hank, following my instructions, originally connected you to the Kirlians. The brain, once it has recorded such a pattern, can never lose it. But it can be told to forget that the programming is there. This is that extra knowledge of hypnotism, which I've already mentioned. For example, when you attached yourself to the mind-expansion machine in Hal's basement, apparently on an impulse, you were carrying out a command that I had given you amnesia on."

"I'm beginning to feel better," said Chip.

"How do you mean?" Surprised tone.

"Thank God, somebody was taking responsibility on this dangerous business long ago."

"There's more, but I'll come to that presently. The key thought is, when emotion intensifies, hypnotism is by-passed. When I increased the power of the mind-expansion machine, your feeling that you had been disconnected from the Kirlians was automatically overwhelmed, and there was the pattern still intact. In the heat of battle, the Ig commander is liable to forget his conditioning; and that's our problem. I really thought I had you where you couldn't possibly do anything before the enemy fleet got here. But, by God, you got those ships up there partially manned. That could nullify a lot of my best-laid plans."

He broke off. "Chip, since you are the person who is connected to this Ig by way of Hal's machine, I'm going to have to withdraw. The battle is basically up to you."

"Wait!" yelled Chip. "What do you mean, battle? I need advice. What do I do?"

The outline of Dr. Frith, which had started to fade, steadied. It stood there. It had a faint smile. "We anarchists," said the psychiatrist, "have always been great proselytizers. If you'll think about it, that's our best weapon. Get the other fellow where he's caught by the same anarchistic limitations that we're caught by. Naturally, one of our tools for achieving such a goal has to be, what we call, the cameraderie of the Kirlians. Every Kirlian knows what every other Kirlian is doing."

Dr. Frith concluded: "As for the battle—remember, the general, who usually operates well to the rear, puts the troops into jeopardy. Their job is to fight their way out. I'm the general, and my rear position is on a fishing vessel somewhere in Antarctica. You're the troops. Good luck!''

''Hey!'' said Chip.

But the ghostly apparition had started to fade again. Moments later, it became one of the colorful flowers. It twinkled orange, red, yellow. And was gone.

TWENTY-NINE

BATTLE?

Chip had climbed to his feet and fumbled his way to a chair at one of the unoccupied tables. He sat with his eyes closed. That was the outer action, the visible "battlefield."

The inner action included the Kirlian colors, and music, and tiny images. In addition was the outline of a face that looked like a cross between a large squirrel and a small horse. The image as he saw it was unfair to the Ig, who was actually quite a handsome, sophisticated individual. But direct vision was never involved in an energy interconnection. The human mind recreated what it saw from personal associations. In this instance, that meant earth creatures.

His hope was that he could penetrate all barriers in both of these universes. The restaurant *and* the inner vision. "Can you hear me, Mr. Ig?" Chip said aloud. He added, "If 'hear' is the right word?"

There was a pause. During that silence, the Slua thought: "If I talk to him, I can, at least, gain time, and at best discover what the threat is, if any."

He thereupon said matter-of-factly in what sounded in Chip's head like North American English: "What you humans have in this Kirlian thing is a mechanical version of a system of mental communication that we call 'lateran unity.' With us it's an organic condition from the earliest days of our evolution.''

Chip was twenty years old; and the fact that he had got an answer exhilarated him. What was happening didn't look like the beginning of a battle. He actually thought: ''Maybe we can both with this war. By straight talk!''

He said ''That startles me, sir. Because it sounds like the best communication system that could possibly be devised.''

''We think so,'' said the Ig, smugly.

''And yet,'' argued Chip, ''you ended up as mass murderers. How could you correlate the two?''

It was straight talk indeed. In all his life the Ig had never been spoken to so bluntly. In a manner of speaking, he gasped at the insult. Then replied icily, ''It would be pointless to go into the underlying philosophy of the realities of the universe.''

''On earth,'' persisted Chip, ''individuals who accidentally have a special ability subsequently construct an entire complex of self-esteem around that one condition. Similarly, persons born to wealth or into an hereditary title, use that as a basis for *their* ego satisfaction. Since anarchism, the so-called harmless people, those who because of a childhood trauma are withdrawn, over-obedient, and otherwise incapable of expressing anger and therefore unable to do violence, have been overheard expressing quiet but total self-congratulatory conviction that their suppressed state proves them to be the real elite. My guess would be that, similarly, the Ig accepted their lateran unity communication ability as proof that they are innately superior to anyone else.''

The conversation was becoming boring as might be expected from the fact that the human involved was but an overgrown child, and therefore not up to an adult realistic dialogue. The Ig said condescendingly, "You will surely grant that your method of speech is better than smoke signals or gestures with fingers."

"Better for whom and for what?" challenged Chip. "In ancient days smoke signals were the only long distance communication system available. Between two deaf mutes, finger gestures are a viable language."

"I can see," said the Ig sarcastically, "that you and I cannot have a logical conversation."

"One more comment," said Chip, "and then I'll ask the big question. The way I see all this—" he went on—"is that individual Ig, motivated much as earth human beings are, to further their own interests, developed methods of concealing their real thoughts. In my early schooling de-sensitization techniques were used to prevent us kids from suppressing our feelings and thoughts on the principle that anything suppressed would eventually make problems. It turns out that sensitivity training doesn't work on kids—they're too sensitive—so we all ended up suppressing our feelings, and continuing to live in a world that has to be monitored by Kirlians. Apparently, *any* concealment leads to something unfortunate, and that's got to be the explanation for why the Ig do what they do. So my big question is—"

"I'm waiting," said the Ig impatiently.

Sitting there at the table, Chip involuntarily drew a deep breath, as he projected the thought: "Is there any chance that we can negotiate the Ig fleet out of the solar system?"

There was no immediate reply, for the simple reason that the innocence of the question . . . so unrealistic . . . left the Ig, in a manner of speaking, speechless.

As Chip waited, he "saw" that the colors streaming past his mind's eye were no longer entirely flower-like. The Kirlian effect, with its enormous diversity, was beginning to come through *as it really was*: the same number of colors, but now the actual basic patterns were there, not one the same.

More—the initial attempt of his brain to force the flower shape having yielded to a partial truth, even a few scenes flickered by at the very edge of his awareness: a street, the front of a house, the hallway of a building. They were views of a small, inhabited portion of a planet's surface: the narrow world of a Kirlian computer. What planet was not obvious to Chip's ability as it was in these still-early stages.

Brief awareness came again of where he was sitting: in the deserted Sub D restaurant, on a bench at one of the long tables. This time, a thought, a puzzlement . . . Hey! when I conked out I was in Lovers Lounge with *her*!

That was all. His first recollection in all these minutes of Leslie.

No other thought. No sense of alarm about her. Continued acceptance that she was safe in a protected area.

At that precise moment, the Ig recovered sufficiently from his incredulity that Chip could have asked so utterly naive a question. "And what," he asked sarcastically, "can you offer on your side of the negotiation?"

There was no immediate reply. The other's hostility had penetrated into Chip's awareness. And it brought the kind of shock that comes to people who for the first time are confronted by a criminal mind. Chip thought blankly: "My God, there is going to be a battle!" The blankness was because he still hadn't the faintest idea what form that battle would take.

The Ig went on in the same dismissing tone: "It is generally agreed that two parties who are negotiating must realistically accept the *status quo* as their starting point. The present situation, I wish to point out, is that within a dozen hours, earth time, we Ig shall have total control of the entire solar system. May I ask—" heavy sarcasm—"what you have to offer over and above *that*?

"Furthermore," the Ig continued, "since I'm the one that has the natural communication ability, at this point I shall use my greater experience to dominate this connection between you and me, and—"

Pause. A distinct mental impression of someone in shock. Then: "Hey!" The Slua sounded querulous. "What's happening?

THIRTY

A FEELING had come to Chip.

It wasn't fear. Because an ex-lieutenant-colonel cannot be afraid.

But he felt himself to be in the wrong location for what was threatening. There was not a single Kirlian in this deserted sub-D world. And his feeling, his purpose, said that the person on whom the safety of earth might well depend ought to be in a protected area. In case something went wrong.

The thought and the action were, almost literally, one. The act of scrambling to his feet, and the immediate launching of his body into a dead run, were equally synchronized, almost blank aspects of a single mind-body coordination.

It was not fear. But it had an amazingly similar physiologic force.

Like emotion, it pre-empted. With the nerve ends of the action centers of the brain firing at high speed, the Ig takeover would have to wait.

—Out the door and along the hallway to those rubber-padded stairs that were designed to save the lives of people who might "accidentally" be pushed down a flight, or two, or three . . . Up those stairs to Level G.

It was presently evident that insect protein was, in fact, a body-building food. He reached Lover's Lounge breathless but viable. And still able to think and do things in sequence. He ran past the Co-op sitting at the entrance desk, and he half-fell on the first settee. He was at this point directly opposite the Kirlian guarding the corridor connecting the Zero Zero community with the lounge.

Safe? Chip didn't think of it in such terms. Still gasping, he identified himself to the Co-op attendant, finishing hastily: "I may be acting very strange during the next half-hour. But no matter how odd it looks, don't move me! Don't call for medical help! And don't pay any attention to the fact that I may be speaking to somebody you can't see. I—"

That was as far as he got. Exactly at that instant, the Ig said coldly into his mind, "You gained a little time there, but it will do you no good."

Chip let himself sag back onto the couch. He said aloud, resigned, "All right. I'm curious. What can Ig organic lateran unity do against the mechanical Kirlian system?"

There was no mental message in reply. But . . . the flower images seemed to become darker. As if the bright colors were being squeezed out of them. Even the already faint musical notes took on a muted tone.

"So that's the method," thought Chip enthralled. "An actual feedback." Earth scientists had experimented greatly, and so far unsuccessfully, to achieve such a reversal. "Maybe, if I observe carefully, I'll be able to see how it's done."

It was pretty basic stuff. All living things *are* energy fields. An actual radiance is emitted by a plant, an area of skin, an eye, *any* surface of a live

223

body. This radiation is called the Kirlian Effect, after its scientific discoverer, and it was first observed when photographed by a special still camera. Later, of course, it could be photographed in motion by way of continuous television as a pattern of changing colors.

The living body in a state of peace and harmony emits one color pattern. That same body, feeling fear, creates a different pattern of colors. And when it feels rage, still another pattern is visible.

It was discovered that computers, monitoring such color changes, could detect the most minute nuances of human emotion. And so could instantly observe *all* variations of intent to violence. With that, it became possible to locate Kirlian monitor posts like street lamps on every block of every city and town. And with that, the anarchistic world became possible.

It was a world in which human beings were free to do anything that did not violate the rights of others. The process was more complex than its optimistic promoters had anticipated. Each year additional harassments by that percentage of human beings who will not let well enough alone, had to be taken into account, and had to be programmed for.

That same human mis-nature still brought rueful head shakes from people. Always, when it seemed as if, finally, everything had been taken into account, suddenly there would be another harassment. Usually, after its potentialies were noticed by some misbegotten brain, it became the current cult madness of the alienated, and swept the wide world. Chip vaguely recalled that the Irritation of the Year—this year—was going up to somebody's mailbox just after the mail was delivered, slitting open his personal letters, and reading what was inside.

Essentially harmless, not at all the same as stealing mail—which *was* programmed against—but definitely an outrageous act. Required, now, would be an enormous programming action by the Techs. And several hundred thousand more offenders sent down the line to the educational community that fitted whatever nonsense was going on in their heads.

THIRTY-ONE

ALOUD, Chip said, "Hey, that is new. By changing the pattern you force another thought or emotion on the victim. Right now, I'm just watching it, but I can sense the beginning of a feeling."

As Chip reached that point in his thought, there was a startled reaction from the Ig. "What did you do?"

"What do you see?" countered Chip.

"A scene. A street."

Pause. "Now, what do you see?"

"Another street. Hey!—" Puzzled—"how are you doing this? I've established dominance, yet we keep shifting."

"It's the mechanical Kirlian thing," Chip explained. "I had to be trained against being automatically shifted, when I was first connected to the Kirlian network. The way this thing between you and me works: each time you try to take over, then for a moment I can no longer do the defensive ritual. Instantly, we do an automatic shift. Momentarily, then, you lose control of me. The shift action stops until you try to dominate again. This could go on the same uncontrollable way indefinitely. But why don't you let me take us aboard one of the earth fleet ships? I'd like to see what's happening."

"How would you do that? Take us to a specific place, I mean," said the Ig trying to sound as if it were a matter of scientific interest to him.

"I detect a sly purpose in your question," responded Chip, cheerfully. "But it's all right. I want your cooperation, although I probably don't need it." He went on, "Each of these Kirlians has its own power source. Each can operate separately on a simple defensive level. Through various Kirlian centers, it knows where the other Kirlians are, and where every human being in the world lives. So long as they're part of a network, all I have to do is either give a street address, or a name, then let go of my control; and I'm automatically shifted to the Kirlian on that street. Naturally, having been aboard one of our warships for years, and intercommunicated with the others, I know the Kirlian signals for all the fleet vessels."

"I don't see how I can stop you from going aboard," confessed the Slua. "From what you say, I deduce that, by constantly trying to control you, I could force a shift every few seconds. That way you could only catch momentary glimpses. At this point I see no point in such an harassment."

In fact—that was his private thought—*every moment that I prolong this is a moment gained for the Ig fleet.*

Chip was speaking: "All right, we'll go there!"

As he said the words aloud, and as he thereupon recalled the coordinates of the great spacecraft that he himself had been aboard for so long, he had a private thought of his own that was not cheerful at all: "Is this the battle? And have I won a meaningful victory by preventing the enemy from controlling me?"

Within instants after he had that thought, the Ig said, "Dr. Frith and you are going to have do better than merely holding me away from you. The decisive factor continues to be that our fleet is presently maneuvering into an orbit around your home planet. And, since there are no Kirlians aboard the Ig ships, there is no way that they can be affected by our little mental game."

"Yeah!" agreed Chip, glumly.

The thought and the feeling receded. He was gazing along a spaceship corridor. And there was no one in sight. Not a movement. Not a sound.

He decided presently: "I suppose I could locate the people aboard."

Since there seemed nothing better to do, and since the Slua was silent and unobtrusive, he shifted to a second Kirlian, then a third, and a fourth, and on. He found a baker's dozen of men in each of three bars being politely served by robot waiters. Another score of men, plus or minus one, were in a theater watching a film showing. Several dozen more were in game rooms, playing tennis or shooting pool. And that was the visible activity.

Presumably, a few of the others were in bedrooms sprawled in the deep sleep of the unwary and the unthinking. Because Kirlians were not located in bedrooms, that part was pure conjecture, of course.

Chip was not discouraged. Being a persistent type, once started, he had his viewpoint switched successively to several of the ship's control centers, in turn. And there was the first significant reward of his patience.

A single individual sat in the captain's chair on the bridge. In front of the man—a bearded type—was a vast, lighted viewplate. Chip glanced at what was visible on that plate; and it was not what it should have been for a vessel in orbit.

It took a while, but presently he realized the somewhat awesome truth. Acting on the instruction of one man, the huge warship had lifted away from its circular course around earth. And it was now on a course that in ten or twelve days would take it out of the solar system.

After making that discovery, Chip grew resigned. One by one he now visually toured each of the remaining fourteen warships. What he found was discouraging—in view of what Dr. Frith had said. Altogether, eleven of the huge craft had left their orbits. In every instance, this had apparently been done on the instruction of one or two persons; two was the maximum number of individuals he found in any control room.

He was still surveying one of the vessels when alarm signals rang out on each of the ships. They sounded, first, softly, in the Captain's great bridge. Then in a rising cacophony the clamor circulated through the ship.

On one level of reality, then, there was no problem. From the beginning the Caps and the Co-ops had taken normal kids of the civilized world between ages ten and sixteen and given them ship, weapon, and ground military training. So everybody aboard had some basic understanding of robot machinery and the ethics of an anarchistic state of war.

In their response to the alarm signals, the alienated extremists aboard earth's fleet ships initially divided into two groups. There were those who were unusually suspicious. They decided instantly that the mechanical screaming and clanking was a trick. Exactly what kind of trick, and by whom instigated, they did not bother to explain either to themselves or to anyone else.

The second group was larger than the first. Each individual of that group had strong survival instincts. As a group they reacted swiftly and determinedly.

Anarchistic space warcraft are programmed. They *can* automatically put up energy defense screens. But they can *not* fire with intent to damage until somebody gives a direct order. They cannot even aim by themselves. The aiming has to be done by human beings. There was an additional restriction: The Kirlians will not allow a human being to aim a lethal weapon at another human being, or at a known anarchistic ally.

On the eleven ships that came back to engage the enemy all necessary communication among personnel took place on intercoms and viewplates. By agreement with the personnel aboard the four ships that had remained in orbit, the battle was scheduled to begin when the first of the eleven arrived. That would be in less than half an hour.

THIRTY-TWO

"DR. FRITH, are you there somewhere?"

Sitting in the Lovers Lounge, eyes closed, Chip spoke the words aloud, anxiously, and added:

"Doctor, they're going to fight; and I don't know how to stop them—if that's what I should do."

There was a pause. Then a faint, faraway voice said, "Chip, this is the situation I tried to avoid. Now, we'll just have to see how it comes out."

"Don't you have any suggestions, sir? And, besides, why shouldn't they fight?"

The faraway voice explained that the giant warcraft were all mined, and could be blown up at will by the enemy. "Maybe they'll do it anyway," said Dr. Frith. "But I have an idea that they'd like to capture the ships intact. And of course, for us, after all this is over, it would be an economic nightmare for Hal to have to try to get the money from the big corporations to rebuild them."

The Ig, who was monitoring the conversation, felt absolutely baffled as those words were spoken. What could justify the confidence that Dr. Frith seemed to have, that there would be a future for mankind?

A moment later Chip uttered the same thought, but in a more desperate tone: "For God's sake, sir, the way this looks to me now is that there's not a single hope visible. Except for you and Hank and Hal and me, nobody knows or cares about this."

"Before I say anything on that, Chip, let me ask

you a question: What major are you planning to take when you start college?''

It was such an unexpected change of subject, so utterly unimportant at this ultimate moment of human history that it had the effect of lightening Chip's spirits. He decided to play the game of life right to the last minute *as a game*.

In that mood, he said cheerfully, ''What do you suggest, Doctor?''

''Chip,'' was the surprisingly earnest reply, ''every generation of anarchists is going to have to have somebody keeping an eye on outer space. A generation ago, when I was a young man, there was an old fellow who selected me to be that person for the then future time when he wouldn't be able to do it. Now, I'm selecting you. So why don't you become a psychiatrist in the modern sense?''

''Well,'' he said doubtfully, ''I'm really not the type that can sit still for hours and listen to other people's problems.''

''That isn't the way things are done, anymore. So, having said that, let me tell you that there *is* one visible hopeful condition. We have the Ig connected to you through that mind-expansion machine.''

Chip protested: ''But he believes he can dominate our connection by a method of continuous harassment.''

''That,'' came the reply, ''is because he's never been the mind-expansion route, Chip. Which is what's going to happen right now, as I turn the power of this machine up to its limit. Good luck, friend.''

''Wait! Is this the battle that you—?''

There was no reply. In words.

THIRTY-THREE

A SCENE . . . of which he seemed to be a part. And, of course, the Ig was also a part of it. Inside a giant star.

He was a tiny point of meaning. It was long, long, long ago. And far away. Oh, so long and so far.

Endless convulsions. No sense of hot or cold, but, around him, movement, movement, movement.

But an instant came when the speed of that movement transformed timelessness into time.

The meaning thing was expelled into a dark emptiness. It broke up into millions and millions of smaller meanings.

At that precise moment began the feeling of loss, of not being whole, of achingly wanting to rejoin and again be a part of a greater whole.

Forever began to go by, one second at a time. All the together feelings continued, but there was presently the *custom* of being separate.

. . . We really belong together, but I wouldn't know how to act if I was once more a part of the basic meaning.

Many, many, many times portions of the original meaning drifted together, And repelled each other. There was a sense of needing, of attraction, and simultaneously of not wanting, of pushing away.

How confused can you be? I want to be free, but I have to belong.

A thought: Basic man has his roots in the belief that everybody is everybody, that everybody owns everything, all women and all men are married to each other—and, deep inside, he has a strong impulse to be, and act, this way. But, of course, that basic is no longer a truth; since he *is* separate, and belongs only to himself. Thus he has to rationalize his impulse, when it manifests, over the dead bodies, so to speak, of those who resist his "rationality."

There were consequences everywhere, everywhere: government, military, police, vigilantes, community protective associations, guards patrolling night and day, the ancient warrior sleeping with one hand gripping his knife and the other his spear, the modern Kirlian computers watching every street with their solid-state programming. . . . The young man—Chip—except for a few minor barriers, was unrestricted, unconditioned, totally free. The minor exception: he was connected to the Slua-Ig. So long as that connection existed, he was not to that extent, at liberty to do as he pleased. But—the connection, of course, worked both ways.

The Slua had watched the fantastic scene with considerable interest, like an objective observer trying to find out what the enemy was up to. At first he scarcely noticed that an unusual thought had come into his mind. He thought, "We are all living creatures of the universe."

It was one of those casual mental things, which he dismissed instantly. But afterwards he reflected scathingly: "Considering all the planets on which we Ig gameplayers have destroyed the dominant species, imagine what would happen if we suddenly

believed they were relatives of ours, however re-
motely."

Fleeting as the thought was it brought a momentary feeling of regret. Which, naturally, he instantly
rejected, characterizing it as "ludicrous."

Simultaneously, he consciously strove to shift his
attention. It was a powerful attempt to dismiss, dis-
engage from, an automatic process.

It worked. After a long moment the Ig realized that
he was having an awareness of how Chip was being
affected by the "mind expansion."

He saw that he was looking at a scene, quite mun-
dane. It showed the girl, Leslie Bjornsen inside a
bedroom with George Tamper. . . .

Several additional moments went by. Realization
of the truth came suddenly. The scene he was looking
at was *not* a Kirlian view. It was inside Tamper's
bedroom, for God's sake! And there were no Kirlians
inside these ordinary sleeping rooms. No protection
there. For anybody.

The Slua deduced what had happened. For Chip
the process of mental expansion had amplified a
natural time cognition. Extrasensory perception! A
hidden human ability of the same type as that by
which he had originally viewed earth through Chip's
nervous system. But a different aspect. Some kind of
return in time to an earlier hour was involved.

The Ig thought: "Chip must have remembered the
girl and wondered about her. Perhaps had even had a
sudden deep-felt anxiety. And this is what happened!"

Chip seemed to be floating near a ceiling. Below
him by a few feet only, was none other than George

Tamper. And, in an easy chair, her legs drawn up defensively, Leslie.

Chip had a strange feeling about the scene. The feeling was that this wasn't happening—not now. It was as if a perpetual mist had cleared from an inner vision, giving him an instant connection to—To what?

The ridiculous impression was that he was gazing at a recreation of something that had once happened. "I did," he remembered, "suddenly think about Leslie. Is this the result of that?"

Even as he felt uncertain of the reality, the girl uttered words that under . . . reality . . . circumstances were obviously a continuation of a dialogue already in process. She said, "Are you sure, Mr. Tamper, that you want to take the risks of doing this?"

She seemed surprisingly calm, and even sounded a little incredulous. It occurred to the watching Chip that people accustomed to the protection provided by Kirlians had not had the opportunity to develop fear.

Leslie went on, "The price may in the long run be higher than you want to pay."

Tamper, who had been smiling, suddenly looked startled. Then he walked—no, half-staggered—to the bed, and sank down on it. "You're doing something to me," he mumbled, "I'm feeling sleepy."

"For my protection," said the girl, "Dr. Frith gave me one of those—you know, it's a hypnotic thing."

"Basically," yawned Tamper, "I can't be hypnotized. But I can go to sleep, and can forget."

"Why don't you go out this other door?"

suggested the girl. "Then I won't have to keep putting you to sleep."

"Yeah, that's a good idea." He slid off the bed to the carpet, and, after swaying there on hands and knees, began laboriously to crawl across the floor.

Leslie called after him, "Will you tell Chip, when he awakens, that Dr. Frith sent an airline ticket with me, for his return home?"

Tamper did not reply. He was fumbling with the latch. When he finally got the door open, it took at least a minute before he made it across the threshold. Only after he was out in the corridor did the girl unwind.

She did it rapidly. And, once on her feet, she ran to the door. She closed and bolted it. Seconds after that, she had also bolted the other door. . . .

The scene blurred suddenly. And from out of the blankness came Dr. Frith's faraway anxious voice, "Chip, for God's sake, you let an emotion pre-empt the battle. Don't do that again! Please! This is a last ditch fight for human existence."

"Sir," said Chip, who was suddenly back in the Lovers Lounge, conscious of the settee pressing against his body; his voice was thick with anguish, "I still don't know what this battle is that you keep referring to."

"Shake him loose, Chip!" The psychiatrist's voice was genuinely frantic. "This Ig has somehow got himself away from his own cellular history. Get him back in there. Keep shifting!"

Chip asked no more questions. A great light had dawned. Of course! Grimly, he shifted . . . from Kirlian to Kirlian to Kirlian. He *felt* the Ig shift with him. He was even aware that it was a conscious effort each time; the enemy was actually, consciously thinking of the shift, and holding his mind on every move with intense concentration.

With that, the desperate youth realized that the mechanical movement was not enough. It was necessary to keep on shifting; but now, with abrupt insight, he began an accompanying verbal patter: "Okay, Mr. Ig, this finally is the battle. And you're really on the spot. It's a battle of words, and of inner truth. The truth is that the Ig derive from—" Sharply—"from where?"

Incredibly, it worked. The surprise yell, demanding the completion of a thought from the Slua. Automatically, the outwitted gameplayer did as was commanded of him.

He thought: . . . Yes, the Ig derived from one bit of the meaning that had been flung out into space on that ancient day of the beginning of life in the universe.

And the human beings derived from another bit of that same source of all life.

THIRTY-FOUR

IT WAS BASIC truth, suddenly breaking through. For that incredible truth to manifest, *billions* of years of amnesia were penetrated.

For the Ig, who was experiencing that "scene" with Chip, the impact was like a physical blow, a blow so hard that it shook him out of a lifetime of conditioning.

The first result was guilt, in waves—we have been exterminating our brothers and sisters. . . .

The feeling was so intense, so encompassing, that in a matter of moments it blew open his contact with the commander of the earth invasion fleet.

"Stop!" the Slua-Ig ordered hysterically. "Do not attack!"

The fleet officer, who had responded courteously to the lateran unity interaction, was surprisingly calm. "Sir," he said, "you must not feel personally threatened by what is happening."

The mentally spoken words were *non-sequitur* enough for the Ig gameplayer to notice vaguely. But he was much too disrupted to react to their odd implication.

The fleet commander continued in a reassuring way: "No one has to die. That's the beauty and perfection of the Kirlian system as it has been developed and used by these earth people. Even the most vicious beings in the entire galaxy, you gameplayers, can be tamed by the method."

The directness of that meaning penetrated through all the passion and the guilt and the confusion.

"What!" said the Slua-Ig. In effect.

"You will be interested to know," said the fleet admiral, "that multi-millions of Kirlians have now been set up on all the Ig planets, including one in every room of the palace of every nobleman. Henceforth, the one emotion which will receive the severest reaction is that associated with any attempt to play games with intelligent beings everywhere. Naturally, on the harassment level, the Kirlians will also react to violence and to the giving of orders, and to other lesser offenses of the hierarchy."

"B-but how was this done?"

"When we boarded those captured earth vessels and discovered how *they* used the Kirlian phenomena, it was apparent that our long search was over."

"What search? What are you talking about?"

"All these decades," was the reply, "while our fleet was invading distant parts of space, we top officers kept hoping that someday we would find a planet whose inhabitants would have some scientific development which we could use to free ourselves and our families at home from the tyranny of the gameplayers. Well, sir—if I may still use that term, possibly for the last time—the anarchistic technology of earth was it. Of course, we needed time to manufacture and install the Kirlian devices. Our trip to earth was the necessary diversionary action, while fleet supply factories were converted to manufacturing Kirlian computers on a mass scale.

"Obviously," concluded the officer, "the Ig workmen in the factories and those who did the installations had no idea what they were for. The whole job was to have been completed today, and the various palaces left to the very end of the project. For secrecy reasons, these final installations could only be entrusted to known and dedicated rebels—and would have to be done by force. So—"

"You mean . . . my palace. Here? Now?"

This time the pause, the sudden doubt, was at the other end of the unity: a startled thought from the admiral.

"You mean—this isn't why you said what you did? The takover hasn't happened yet?"

It had taken a while, but the Slua-Ig was back to normal. All the barriers were back in place, nullified by the unexpected direction of the conversation. "I haven't the faintest idea what you're talking about," he said coldly. "You don't seem to realize that you have probably been the victim of subtle suggestions made through the Kirlian network by Dr. Alan Frith. You will at once hand over command of the fleet to—"

Something struck the steel door of the science room with all the force of a battering ram. One hinge screeched loose with a metallic whining sound, and the door leaned slightly inward. As the startled Ig turned to face the source of the interruption, there was a second smashing blow. This time the door was lifted with a sharp cracking noise, and flung into the room.

It hit the padded floor with a thud, bounced, fell over once, and lay still.

The machine that now rolled through the open door was mounted on large, rubber-like wheels. The armored front of it was about six foot high, and three feet wide. The machine continued to push through the door opening. At least eight feet of armored length entered, and then there were the rear wheels.

The mobile unit glided all the way in and made a wide turn. As it did so, its rear was revealed to have an attachment: two metal vises. These held a long metal pole—perhaps ten feet long and five inches wide.

The length of the pole turned out to be adjustable. The "tank" backed into a corner, and there some mechanical manipulation braced the lower end of the pole against the floor, and adjusted the upper end until it pressed firmly against the ceiling. At which point, the vises let go.

At once, leaving the pole in position, the armored vehicle headed for the door, went through it, and was then visible heading along the wide hallway.

During an early stage of the invasion, the astounded Ig baron made an attempt to achieve a lateran unity with whoever was inside the tank. There was a mind there, but it refused his communication.

The Slua thereupon sought contact with the captain of his guard—*and was refused the connection*. It required about a minute to discover that not one of the top people of his province would talk to him.

Suddenly, he realized what had happened: I have had a Kirlian computer placed near me. Wherever I go, there will be others watching. . . .

Because he was, after all, a great Ig, with millions of the neural circuits of his brain reflecting memories of power, courage, leadership, slyness, and murder, the Slua now grew calm.

Suddenly, he was thinking again, reasoning, considering. And so, within the frame of the lateran unity he was able to say frankly, "I can't quite believe the Kirlian control on the Ig planets is a totally established as you say. And as for the situation in the solar system—"

He was interrupted, hurriedly: "Excuse me, former excellency, we're about to be attacked by the earth fleet, and—"

"I was about to say," said the Ig gameplayer, "those alienated human beings on board those ships may not be numerous, but presumably Antarctica is as low as they go before starting to fight for survival. You will now have to blow up the earth fleet to save yourself."

"Former excellency—"

The great Ig continued as if he had not heard the interruption, on a hopeful note: "It may even be, for your own survival, you will have to destroy earth itself."

"As I was about to say, former excellency," came the reply, "our solution will be evasive action, not fighting. Since they can only shoot if we strike first, it should not take too long before they realize our peaceful intentions. We may need some help in establishing anarchism, and so we plan to make contact with Dr. Alan Frith and perhaps other leaders. As for your own situation, I repeat, don't worry! You still own all your property. Bearing that in mind, even those of your wives who hate you the most probably won't leave right away. And the truth is, it's best for everybody that there be no rapid changes. Goodbye, former sir. Next time I see you it will be as an equal. I am disconnecting."

The ignoble Ig nobleman had the odd, reassuring realization that he was, in fact, being treated courteously. And that was significant. Because for the first time in the history of Ig it was not part of an enforced ritual, but was freely offered.

THIRTY-FIVE

MID-AFTERNOON, Antarctica time.

The young couple walked along the brightly lighted corridor behind a line of girls and women. All were heading toward a door that led outside, where the daily magnetic jet waited. The women were passed through rapidly; but as the couple came up the uniformed man standing there gave the youth a sharp look, and then said, "You really want to test this?"

Chip grinned, turned to Leslie, and said, "This guy doesn't seem to trust the Kirlians to do their job." He pointed back down the corridor about ten feet. "That's one right over there, isn't it?"

The gate guard, who wore the insignia of a Cap Tech, acknowledged reluctantly, "Yes, that's one."

The way he held himself, and his tone of voice, indicated that he was not happy with a male departing on a plane that, shortly before, had brought a load of Lovers Lounge females for that night, and would shortly leave with the female complement of the night before. But he asked for Chip's ticket, and, when he had it, stood for many seconds scowling down at it.

Chip said, "I expect that Kirlian to do its job without fear or favor—as they used to say—and as you can plainly see."

244

"Eh?" A frown, as the man, a stocky type made massive by his winter clothing, glanced up, puzzled. "How do you mean?"

"I trusted you with my ticket."

And *that* remark didn't go over well, either. "Just a minute," said the guard curtly. "Will you two step over here out of the way?" he said, adding, "I seem to recall there's a seventy-five dollar advance payment made by a Captain Latrille." Having spoken the words, he turned, and went through a side door.

A second guard, who had been standing to the rear, now came forward, and checked out several girls and women, barely glancing at their tickets.

Leslie was studying her watch. "It's even closer to take-off time than it was half an hour ago when I was urging you to hurry." She looked and sounded unhappy. "Do you think he really would try to keep you here by a tricky delaying tactic?"

"If he wants to pay the price," shrugged Chip.

They had been standing, facing in the direction they were planning to go. Intent. A little unhappy as the seconds hurried by. Chip's cheerful smile began to look strained.

Suddenly, a hand grasped his shoulder from behind. The youth did not jump or show surprise. Instead, he turned in his best deliberate fashion. But Leslie had already swung around. And it was she who delightedly cried out, "Dr. Frith!"

As Chip completed his turnabout, the first individual he saw was not the physican but a grinning Hank, who said, "Look, when we get back, I'll be moving out of your sister's place—she'll be glad to know." He added, "Now that the big job is done, it's back to Hal for me. Which means I move into a small hotel next to a phone that he can call me on.''

"I guess I'll be moving out of my sister's also,'' said Chip. ''For at least one day I plan to be a good Christian.'' He grinned at Leslie.

At that point, Dr. Frith, who had been glancing back and forth between Chip and Leslie, on the one hand, and the gate attendant, on the other, said, ''Don't let them hold you up much longer, Chip! See you.''

He was starting past when Chip abruptly said, ''How did you get away from that four-day job in one day?''

''We had him sign a release,'' said the psychiatrist in an even voice. Once more, jovially, he clapped Chip on the shoulder. ''Look, friend, don't let these small tricks put you into any anxiety about the future of anarchism. What Leslie did to Tamper, Hank and I did a variation of to a certain Captain. Such things have to be secrets, so they remain small and unobtrusive. If someone, or a group, suspects, you know as well as any living person what can happen.''

This time when the older man started forward, followed by Hank, Chip let them go. Simply stood silently watching as the two men were accepted without argument. They walked off through the door, and disappeared.

The world felt suddenly emptier.

The girl said, ''Ever since I can remember, there's been a rumor that Tech A's have some kind of control over Kirlians, and may not have to pay the price.''

''In that case,'' said Chip, ''we'd better get aboard.'' He started forward. At once, the second guard put out his hand. ''You can't go out this door without a ticket.''

"Who says so?"

"The Kirlian over there." The man pointed.

"Alright. Then you step aside, and let the Kirlian handle the situation. And when your friend comes out with my ticket, ask him to bring it aboard, will you? Come along, Leslie!"

Guard Number Two, a younger man, must have had faith in the Kirlian system, because he made no further effort at delay. They walked through the door, and out into the snow; and the Kirlian did nothing.

"I keep having a hard time with Tech A's and B's," said Chip through the hoarfrost that was already forming on the collar of George Tamper's overcoat, which he wore over George Tamper's best suit. "If anybody has power in an anarchistic society, they have. And you can sense their awareness of it every time you talk to one of them."

"You're a good example yourself," said the girl, her color high from either the extreme cold or the emotion behind the words. They were walking up the ramp. "You ought to be ashamed of yourself for using your power over the Kirlians to steal that man's clothes."

"Does that critical remark mean you're going to refuse to be married to me while I got to college?"

"No, I'm not going to refuse to marry you.'

"Then we can discuss it calmly. I think the price is right. When I find my girl locked in George's room—"

"I locked myself in."

"After George's gang raped her—"

"It didn't happen."

"It's the intent that counts. So I get his rags."

There was another man in uniform standing inside

the outer door of the plane. "Your tickets, please?" he said courteously.

Leslie handed hers over. "Seat number seventeen," said the clean-shaven young man. He thrust the ticket back into her hand, and turned to Chip, questioningly.

Chip pointed. "That a Kirlian just behind you there?"

Without glancing back, the man said, "Yep."

"In its presence," Chip said cheerfully, "and with full awareness of how it would react to a lie, I testify that I have a ticket, and that the gate guard will be bringing it aboard in a few minutes." He concluded, "My seat number is sixteen."

Leslie had already gone on. Chip followed her into the warm, brightly lighted main cabin, where he was one of three male passengers among nearly eight hundred women and girls, all of whom, including Chip, were living evidence that the colossal anarchistic complexity known as the human brain, can adjust to any system, and in the long run survive anywhere.

Because somewhere in a human head, behind all that bright perception, sits a tiny, god-like awareness center, constantly striving to make all the madness work.

And succeeding. Enough.